The Curtain Between Us

Jenny Liang

Potter's Wheel Publishing House
Minneapolis

The Curtain Between Us
by Jenny Liang

Published by POTTER'S WHEEL PUBLISHING HOUSE
MINNEAPOLIS
MN 55378

www.POTTERSWHEELPUBLISHING.com

© 2025 Jenny Liang

All rights reserved. No part of this publication may be reproduced, stored in a retrieval system, or transmitted, in any form or in any means – by electronic, mechanical, photocopying, recording or otherwise – without prior written permission, except as permitted by U.S. copyright law.
For permissions contact:
info@POTTERSWHEELPUBLISHING.com

ISBN: 978-1-950399-24-6

LCCN: 2025940496

Table of Contents

Foreword i

Preface v

Timeline of the Manuscripts ix

Map of the Events, Former North America x

The Song of the Broken xi

Introduction: The Curtain, A.D. 33 1

Chapter One: A Narration from the Voiceless, A.D. 2100 7

Chapter Two: The Origins of a Child, A.D. 2550 10

Chapter Three: The Egyptian, 1930 B.C. 15

Chapter Four: Realities of Divorce, A.D. 1990 18

Chapter Five: Antics of the Unfortunate, A.D. 2540 28

Chapter Six: Rituals and the Like, A.D. 2552 40

Chapter Seven: The Pain of Living, A.D. 1995 48

Chapter Eight: Tragedy in Mizpah, 982 B.C. 54

Chapter Nine: Mother and Son, A.D. 2552 61

Chapter Ten: The Verdict, A.D. 2555 71

Chapter Eleven: Calling, A.D. 2000 80

Chapter Twelve: A Mother's Love, A.D. 2556 87

Chapter Thirteen: The Deception of Women, 3500 B.C.? 91

Chapter Fourteen: Judgment, A.D. 2555 97

Chapter Fifteen: Peace at Last, A.D. 2007 103

Chapter Sixteen: Warmth, A.D. 2558 106

Chapter Seventeen: A Case Study, Translated into
Twenty-First-Century English Vernacular, A.D. 3508 112

Acknowledgments 115

DEDICATION

To Dr. Adina Kelley, who passed after a difficult battle with colon cancer. It was your classes that sparked my love for the human story, planting a seed of hope inside me for writing. I miss you every day, and I wish you were here to see the multitude of flowers that now bloom through your passionate devotion to your students. Your bravery amidst the turmoil of the world brightly shines throughout this book.

FOREWORD

At a time when our country is polarized between left and right and we versus they, it is rare to read a story that questions everything you believe, everything you were taught, and everything you thought you knew. *The Curtain Between Us* asks, "Are you absolutely, positively sure you know what you're talking about? Do you actually believe what you say you believe?" We are often so confined in our way of thinking that to us, our beliefs and moral compasses are the absolute truth. We are in the right, and everyone else is wrong. There is no higher power except humanity—or, more specifically "me." *The Curtain Between Us* throws all those clichéd ideas out the window.

The author starts with the crucifixion of Christ and ends up hundreds of years in the future, but it's not a linear journey. The story moves forward and backward through human history by taking place in a futuristic Christian dystopia, a mysterious past, and an uncertain present (whenever that may be). All of us, at one time or another, tend to question how we were brought up and what we were led to believe. *The Curtain Between Us* brings these questions to light as the reader delves into the story.

Despite her young age, the author can effectively relate these life struggles, conflicts, and questions to the reader. Jenny Liang is one of those rare people who personally understands the struggles of faith, duty to family, devotion to self, and the eternal question of "How do I fit into all of this?" She has accomplished more at the age of 20 than most of us could ever think of doing in our lifetimes.

A graduate of the University of Northwestern, a published poet, and a writer, director, and composer of a short film, Jenny already seems to have accomplished all she can. But as *The Curtain Between Us* illustrates, a person's role in the world constantly changes, and she is not content to stay the same, yet she is uncertain what her next steps should be. Readers will wonder how much and what sections of *The Curtain Between Us* are actually biographical rather than fiction.

Over the years, I have met some really remarkable people. As a state senator, I've hired many interns during my tenure, and they truly become a part of my staff even though they only work for me during the four- to five-month legislative session. Rarely have I met an intern with such a giving heart who aims to please everyone she meets yet strives for personal, academic, and professional excellence. Jenny constantly looks for ways to expand her experiences and add to her already vast knowledge. A journey that she asks the reader to join with her. So, what is this "curtain" between us? Was it the curtain that was torn in two when Christ died on the cross, breaking the barrier between us and God? Does the curtain hide our deepest fears or pique our curiosities? Who is behind it? What can we learn from it? Why do we seek it? What does the curtain do to us as a society?

The Curtain Between Us reflects Christianity, philosophy, human emotions, and our need to connect with something bigger than ourselves. There are obvious continuities within this book, such as certain phrases and biblical names. However, the underlying theme of *The Curtain Between Us* is facing the very basics of human emotions: the fears of being alone and living a life that has no purpose—at least not one known to us.

The Curtain Between Us is a "read more than once" type of a book. When you read it a second time, you may want to read it in chronological order to see if your perceptions have changed. Regardless, *The Curtain Between Us* is written by a very talented young woman who leaves us with many unanswered questions but one common theme:

Have mercy on me.

State Senator Gary Dahms represents Senate District 15, in southwestern Minnesota. When he is not working at the capitol in St. Paul, Senator Dahms lives in Redwood Falls with his wife of 50 years, Barb. He has two grown children, Michelle (husband Byron) and Michael; and two grandchildren. He is also an active member of the First United Methodist Church in Redwood Falls, Minnesota.

PREFACE

For all who are lost in the journey of life, perplexed about the existence and morality of God, and those wanting to understand the value of being human.

We yearn, arms stretched wide and hearts longing, to connect with a Higher Power. But, it feels so distant. The heat of the Almighty fades in its journey to reach us, yet we are so cold, yearning for his warmth.

But nonetheless, we continue to dream, hoping that one day our hearts will finally connect, beating in one pulse with the Creator.

If I am killed simply for living, let death be kinder than man.

—Althea Davis

TIMELINE OF THE MANUSCRIPTS

3500 B.C.?
DECEPTION IN THE GARDEN
— The Fall of Mankind Begins under Lilith and Nehushtan

An Egyptian is saved, alongside her child, by an archangel
— **1930 B.C.** THE EGYPTIAN IN THE WILDERNESS

982 B.C.
THE SACRIFICE OF A DAUGHTER
— Iphis, the only child and daughter of Jephthah, is sacrificed in Mizpah

Hannah's world falls apart after the dissolution of her personal life
— **A.D. 1990** BREAKING DAWN

A.D. 2007
THE CURTAIN
— Hannah reaches her destination

Hare and Tamar raid the Remnant, Hare encounters Nehushtan
— **A.D. 2552** THE ATTACK

A.D. 2555
VERDICT OF A LOST SOUL
— After the attack of the Remnant, Hagar enters her initiation and encounters a strange boy

One person returns to the Farmhouse inhabited by Tamar decades prior, where a mysterious guest emerges
— **A.D. 2558** PEACE AT LAST

MAP OF THE EVENTS
FORMER NORTH AMERICA
THE MEADOWS
HANNAH'S HOMETOWN
THE FARMHOUSE
FELINE'S DWELLING
VAGABOND DWELLINGS
DESTROYED LANDS
THE REMNANT
THE VISION

the song of the broken

For Voice and Piano   darkness ebbs in   Jenny Liang

dancing across ... pulsing out as

I call ... to you ... waiting

Introduction:
The Curtain, A.D. 33

"And behold, the curtain of the temple was torn in two, from top to bottom. And the earth shook, and the rocks were split."

—Matthew 27:51 (ESV)

A.D. 33 – Golgotha, Historic Palestine

The day was scorched and the sun merciless. Mary Magdalene, eyes swimming with tears, collapsed in agony as her Savior staggered past. Blood and rotting flesh mingled in the dry air with manure, sweat, and palpable fear. *What a damned smell.*

The women huddled together, united in the misery of being born as women in first-century Palestine, unable to intervene during their Savior's crucifixion. They held Mary, mother of the Nazarene, whose ragged frame was wracked from weeping. What's more, the apostles had abandoned their Lord and fled. Now the women were alone, at the mercy of the enraged crowd.

Mary Magdalene, arms still gripped around the Mother, painstakingly hauled them both up the rugged Hill of Golgotha. Rocks crumbled beneath their feet as the dry dust blinded their eyes and choked their parched throats. Mary Magdalene heaved, retching from the stench, her sweaty veil obstructing her already limited line of vision.

Behind their doomed procession lay the city of Jerusalem, bustling with merchants and travelers. In front was her Lord, shaking as the nails were driven into his lacerated body.

As the women dragged the thrashing Mother, desperately fighting and clawing for her dying son, Mary Magdalene locked eyes with her Savior.

His glazed eyes bore into her own, bringing back memories of long ago, when she spent her days terrorized by demons, a mindless agent of Legion's will.

As Magdalene's mind wandered aimlessly past the heaving ropes lifting the crucified upright, she pondered her life as a possessed woman, an outcast among her community, a shame to her people.

Mary Magdalene had grown up on the windy shores of Magdala, a bustling Jewish port city docked with boats carrying fresh fish from the Sea of Galilee. Whenever she wasn't occupied, the young girl would sneak to the Migdal Synagogue and breathlessly glide her fingers across the

Magdala Stone, carved with intricate designs from Solomon's temple. The bases and pillars were so tangibly ethereal compared to the Second Temple in Jerusalem, where YHWH's glory was confined by Roman battalions and crippling taxation.

One day, after being mocked by an inspecting soldier, Mary's uncle had suddenly snapped, lunging and striking the man before being bayoneted by a nearby commander. Mary, who was nearby, ran to her uncle and held him as he bled out in her arms. His knuckles gripped her girl's arm, squeezing so tight a trickle of blood flowed down Mary's elbow.

His eyes stared imploringly before another spear penetrated his body. Mary screamed as life drained from his eyes. She was pushed away, the infuriated soldiers kicking and throwing stones at his corpse.

After the sun set, she returned to view his desecrated body. Everything seemed so dark and empty, void of life or meaning. In an effort to reduce suspicion from the authorities, her parents forbade their children from mentioning their uncle. But Mary would be tormented by his dead eyes, which seemed to follow her wherever she went.

Help me, he would whisper to Mary. *They're hurting me.* As time went on, the girl became engulfed with feelings of rage, extending past her fragile frame and burrowing into her mind. Everything seemed so dark and empty, void of life or meaning. The anger became unbearable and, to alleviate the torture, Mary began to inflict horrific wounds on herself. Her family sent for doctors, but her thrashing and tortured wails drove them away. The religious leaders ordered her to be physically removed from Jerusalem. Thrown outside the city gates, estranged from the synagogues and her beautiful Magdala stone, Mary became truly alone.

Scavenging for scraps and sleeping in ruins led her to a savage and desolate existence. The girl's mind became filled with visions, and not even sleep could provide sanctuary from her demons. Her nightmares were filled with inescapable rituals of murder, and however hard she thrashed, she could not rid herself of her awaiting fate. In these tortured dreams, the religious leaders circled her, eyes filled with malice and disgust. *Demons! The girl is possessed by evil spirits!*

"No! I'm guiltless!" Mary would scream for mercy from the men, pleading her innocence. Circling her, invisible to the spectators, were seven demons, each eyeing her with false pity.

"Kill her!" the religious leaders yelled. Amidst the furious roar from the crowd, Mary attempted to run, but her body was restrained with a rope. Bracing herself, Mary thrashed about as she was pummeled with stones. Each stone felt like a branding iron, searing through her flesh. Then she heard a familiar voice. As the girl whipped around, she would come face-to-face with the murderous face of her uncle. His bleeding body tensed with rage as he heaved a large stone at her.

And each night, Mary Magdalene would wake up

screaming.

When she awoke, shaking in fear, she would feel their presence soothing her. They wrapped themselves over her, covering her like a warm blanket.

The world has abandoned you, but we will never leave you.
Join us and you will never feel alone again.

Mary Magdalene spent years in this tortured existence, caught between the physical world and her spiritual masters. Her body was an agent that she had no power over, and one night, as she plodded up the Mount of Olives, her feet brought her towards the edge.

Hundreds of cubits below her was a rocky outcropping. In the distance appeared the Holy City. And behind her were the graves of her ancestors. As she stared into the void, her voices whispered again.

We'll keep you company. It'll be over soon. We promise.

They began to embrace her shivering body. Mary closed her eyes. She took a deep breath and hovered. But then, as quickly as they entered her years ago, the demons fled in fear, shrieking and plunging into the abyss.

A force pushed the woman back, slamming her against the rocky outcropping of the ridge behind her. Mary lurched into a fetal position as her body became racked with a burning. fire that spread through her limbs, then her brain. She attempted to scream, but nothing came out. The flames seared through her consciousness and being. Then, as suddenly as it had appeared, the pain stopped.

As her vision cleared, Mary Magdalene met the eyes of

her Savior. A soothing warmth spread through her throbbing body as the man smiled softly, his extended hand suspended in the frigid night.

Follow me, he whispered.

And she did.

As her mind returned to the present, Mary and the other women formed a protective barrier around the Mother, shielding the matriarch from her son's corpse. The scorching afternoon was now dark and frigid. Facing them was Jesus the Nazarene, his bloodied body lifelessly suspended on the cross. Her Savior's eyes blankly stared past her.

Behind the group, the city of Jerusalem released a deep groan of agony, audible from beyond the city gates.

The Curtain! she heard. *The Curtain has been torn!*

Adonai, have mercy.

The Curtain of the Holy of Holies was torn.

Chapter One:
A Narration from the Voiceless, A.D. 2100

"I know not with what weapons World War III will be fought, but World War IV will be fought with sticks and stones."

—Albert Einstein

A.D. 2100 – Philadelphia, USA

The cat lived a peaceful existence. Each morning, he would awaken to the sun's warm rays bathing over his aching body. The feline would yawn, exposing his fangs to the lifeless stuffed toy that was carefully placed over his bed. He would then stretch his body and prance to his master's room.

Every day, the cat would communicate his existential need for nutrients until the human stumbled out of bed and made his way into the kitchen. Like clockwork, the mysterious object wielded by his owner produced a terrific sound that made every hair on the creature's back perk up.

Food, food, food!

The plop and clinking of the bowl being placed on the floor brought immense joy to the cat.

Each morning, the feline would wrap his furry body around his owner's legs. His eyes narrowed as his master sat in front of a giant box, gripping a strong-smelling foul liquid, and made the box glow with different colors.

What interesting powers these two-legged creatures possessed!

As the mornings passed, the man grew more agitated, palpable fear radiating off his body. The noises released from the magical box became more frantic. Each time, a familiar symbol would flash on the box:

NUCLEAR WAR.

Of course, the cat did not possess the ability to read. But it could detect the fear of his owner, who no longer exited their dwelling place. Food became rationed as well, and the normally bustling streets were silent.

Then, one morning, chaos erupted. The streets thronged with humans and strange metal objects with wheels that his owner would climb into each morning. The owner began to cram all his possessions into a strange box, stopping frequently to tear at his face.

The cat's meows of inquiry were ignored.

His master finally picked him up, tears sliding down his face. "I'm sorry," he whispered. "I can't bring you."

"We're being bombed."

With that, the cat was ceremoniously carried outside as

his owner climbed into the metal object and whisked away, never to be seen again.

A day later, the world erupted in nuclear explosions. When the radiation and heat cleared, shadowy imprints spanned across the nations.

There was no sign of life.

Chapter Two:
The Origins of a Child, A.D. 2550

"The world is a train that's speeding into the abyss, meaning it's descending down. We are also riding that train, though we're staying in the last car."
—Yoelish Kraus

A.D. 2550 – Former Pikes Peak, Rocky Mountains

The girl grew up with stories about the end of the world, wildly elaborate tales about the former hedonistic civilization filled with every vile sin imaginable. How there were powerful machines that operated on witchcraft, which allowed humans to fly and travel faster than any animal.

Humans had turned away from God, just like the original woman, Eve. Without her, the man would have continued to dwell in paradise in the presence of God. But her feminine evils had tempted herself and her husband into sin.

Just like the sorceress Eve, women had led the second downfall of mankind, producing the most vile of sins that led to a near complete eradication of the human race. Outside of their enclave were only charred remains of the former world, burned alongside their sins.

As the girl would shiver in fear, her father would soothe her. *There's nothing scary out there,* he would murmur. *Only some of the survivors of the eradication, who live cursed lives among the rubble.*

Their own people had survived this destruction by living in isolation, largely cut off from human interaction. The initial days were filled with uncertainty, given the fact that much of their community suddenly died or were prone to long bouts of distress until their body collapsed from within.

It was women who caused this destruction, and many women died as a result of their sin or bore stillborn offspring. Hagar's own mother, her father explained, was cursed by sin and bore only daughters. Each was named from the Holy Book, shadows of the women who walked the Earth millennia prior: Mary, Joanna, Esther, Rebekah, Abigail, Dorcas. Although blessed enough to bear offspring, her mother was corrupted by the sin of Eve, a sin so great that she died giving birth to her seventh daughter. Her father named her Hagar because she was yet another daughter, an Egyptian in a family of Israelites.

What's an Egyptian? Hagar asked.

Her father shushed her and continued.

The members had fled deep into the wilderness, losing many of their people until one night, they entered a large clearing with a deep ravine. Across the chasm, a large curtain loomed, spanning most of what the naked eye could visualize. As Hagar listened in awe, her mind envisioned the weary men and women stumbling into their future homes, amazed at the splendid beauty of their surroundings.

Her ancestors.

Light wrapped itself around the magnificent curtain, which possessed intricate designs of the cherubim and seraphim. Strange symbols were etched across its rich red and blue hues, and there seemed to be a radiance emanating from the object.

As her father got to this stage, the girl's amber eyes gleamed. "I know what happens next!"

Her father rustled her wavy brown hair. "It's prayer time," he stated.

Hagar followed her sisters outside, their heads wrapped in clumsily hemmed fabric, and they joined their community as they walked a path worn through by thousands of souls over the centuries.

Hagar closed her eyes and plodded along by memory, the path etched into her brain. On either side of her stood tall trees, arched out and intertwining hundreds of feet above. Birds rustled, and the delighted screams of children were gently hushed.

As the sun began to shine on her face, she opened her eyes. The Curtain stood across the bottomless ravine, surrounded by foggy clouds. Below the cliff, red rocks and parched grass spotted a snowy embankment. Dreamy snowcapped mountains spotted the countryside. Hagar gazed in awe, imagining the surprise and wonder the first settlers of the Remnant must have experienced.

She studied the Curtain more deeply, the velvets intertwined with maroon red and royal blue fabrics. In the distance, there were gold specks along the gold pillars. *Cherubim*, she mouthed. *Angels*.

Tearing her eyes from the Curtain, Hagar saw that her father followed the men in front, so she joined her sisters gathered with the other children. The men gathered nearest to the edge, while the women spread out behind their husbands. The children, a stone's throw away from their mothers, were separated by gender.

Hagar followed her older sisters as they kneeled prostrate on the smooth stone. There were indents in the rock, and Hagar imagined her dead mother kneeling where she kneeled, breathless and in communion. *Mother, can you hear me? What am I supposed to feel?*

She closed her eyes and placed her head on the warm stone. "Jesus, Son of David, have mercy on me," she repeated softly. Murmurs arose around her. "Jesus, Son of David, have mercy on me. Jesus, Son of David, have mercy on me." They gradually escalated into wails and mutterings unintelligible to the girl, which frightened her. Her sisters continued to kneel and whisper. "Jesus, Son of David, have mercy on me." *Am I supposed to feel this broken?*

She remembered the words of her father: "The Curtain is a symbol of our wickedness and God's separation from mankind and eradication of most of the human race. We were spared by his mercy, and this Curtain is a symbol of the distance between our cursed souls and his Presence."

As the sun rose and the wails became more desperate and forced, the girl willed herself to feel taken over by the Spirit. As the children began to sway, she copied their motions and begged to be like them.

Hagar felt nothing.

Nothing.

Chapter Three:
The Egyptian, 1930 B.C.

"And the land of Judah will bring terror to the Egyptians; everyone to whom Judah is mentioned will be terrified, because of what the LORD Almighty is planning against them."

—Isaiah 19:17 (NIV)

1930 B.C. – Wilderness of Paran – Modern-day Sinai Peninsula

Have mercy on me. The Egyptian staggered under the unforgiving heat of the sun, her thoughts slurring under dehydration. She gripped her whimpering child, whose dry skin cracked under his shallow breaths. The flask to which she clung had long since run out of water. On the edge of her vision, the woman spotted vultures slowly advancing, waiting for her to collapse.

Swallowing back tears, the slave woman forced one foot in front of the other, locking her knees to keep them from buckling. "يا إلهي، ساعدني" she whispered. His weak cries and burning face pierced into her soul. The child's breathing was too shallow, his heartbeat becoming harder to detect. The mother, overwhelmed by countless generations of motherly instinct, sank to her knees, being careful not to crush her child, and let out a soundless, anguished wail to the gods.

The mother carefully placed her child, whose chest no longer rose and fell, under the shade of a scrub and kissed him one last time. She then staggered away until she could no longer see her dying son, falling to her knees upon the harsh cropping. Pressing her face to the ground, she closed her eyes.

The momentary darkness within her emerged into a bright light, an unknown force seeping through the hidden crevices of her soul, bringing warmth into the darkness of mortality. The woman felt an indescribable connection to the Divine, the presence of the unimaginable. "Oh," she breathlessly whispered, "have mercy on me."

The Presence, in a transcendent language, wrapped itself around her, transplanting the intensity of heat into her quivering body, revitalizing the woman. In the brief encounter, over a thousand words were transmitted through the Divine and the moral, and an intangible understanding was reached.

She would not know the fate of her child, who would be considered the forefather of billions. None of that mattered to her.

She was a mother, an unexplainable concept ingrained into every fiber of her being, present since the conception of mankind and prevailing past the destruction of the material world.

The Egyptian breathed her appreciation, prostrating herself in submission.

Chapter Four:
Realities of Divorce, A.D. 1990

"God is dead. God remains dead. And we have killed him. Yet his shadow still looms. How shall we comfort ourselves, the murderers of all murderers? What was holiest and mightiest of all that the world has yet owned has bled to death under our knives; who will wipe this blood off us? What water is there for us to clean ourselves?"

—Frederick Nietzsche, *The Gay Science*

A.D. 1990 – Minneapolis, USA

"Never forget what he did to us. Never!" The door slammed, wheels screeched down the driveway, and glass shattered as Hannah's mother hurled vases and figurines to the floor.

Hannah cried, burrowing her body into a fetal position under her bed frame. Rocking back and forth, she pressed her palms against her ears and breathlessly chanted a whispered song over and over.

Dancing across, darkness ebbs in, pulsing out as I call to you, waiting…

Visceral screams emerged from downstairs, her mother mourning the end of a rocky marriage built on professed love that nonetheless crumbled. Hannah had been raised with parents who loathed the sight of each other but stayed for their daughter, a bitter duty that left the child with a fear of love, scars that seemed to only lead to further pain and betrayal.

Nonetheless, the girl, a sensitive and quiet soul, never became accustomed to the aftermath of her parents' arguments, flinching every time she dabbed ointment over the bloodied face of her mother and avoiding her father for days afterward.

"Hannah," her parents used to tell her teasingly, "our miracle child, a daughter given to us by prayer. Do you know why we named you Hannah?"

"I know! I know!" Hannah would exclaim, snuggling into her mother. "Because God answered your prayers with me!"

Laughing, her dad stroked her head, and Hannah would temporarily forget suppressed memories of her father with bloodshot eyes, reeking of alcohol, and her mother's bruises, observed by the cautious girl despite her best attempts to cover the bloated purple marks.

"Just like Hannah," her mom murmured, "your father and I prayed for a child. We made a promise to God before you were born."

"What promise did you make?" Hannah asked.

"Oh," her dad said "you won't understand."

Although Hannah was taken to church every Sunday and excelled in her studies, the young girl would delay returning home until the inevitable darkening of the sky, spending hours of refuge each afternoon in the library, immersing herself in fantasies of a better world—one where she did not feel so miserable in a broken home.

Hannah would forgo the newer books with sleek colors and glossy pages, walking instead through aisles of antique books, her fingers gliding over the old and cracked spines, breathing in the aroma of dusty pages and ink. She would ponder the lives of the authors, lost in time but remembered by their work.

More often than not, her fingertips would pause at the same book, the covers barely bound together, the pages yellowed, and much of its ink unintelligible. Hannah, who was still in primary school, had a difficult time understanding the words. The title, however, was easy to read.

The Curtain.

"Curtain," she whispered. "How strange."

The cover was faded, and Hannah could not tell if there was an image or even a specific color. It was the pictures and words inside the pages that called to her.

> *People throughout history have struggled with the concept of a higher deity, and the nature of that deity. Every folk culture and nation has a history of folk religions, often encompassing the same themes of an afterlife, expectations for societal*

behaviors, and rituals that were expected to appease the Divine. Humankind has always been barbaric, and many expected their gods to have barbaric demands for earthly favors, such as self-mutilation, the destruction of other nations, and both animal and child sacrifices.

Nonetheless, it is the distance between mankind and the Divine that remains an essential question about the nature of man. There seems to be an emptiness, a desperation that consistently drives mankind to establish deities, to seek spiritual powers. In a world with bloodshed and uncertainties, the presence of a higher power seems to bring comfort and assurance that the pains of life are not a wasted endeavor.

Whatsoever, the problem of suffering seems to continually haunt people of religion. If God is good, why does he allow and seemingly permit suffering? This, my readers, leads to only one conclusion: God is dead. God remains dead. And we have killed him.

Although many of the words were difficult to read for a ten-year-old, Hannah was fascinated by the elegant loops and curves of the letters. And the last part! It seemed forbidden, bringing chills the first time she read it. Hannah looked around in fear, making sure no one saw her with the book. She whispered an apology to God, half expecting to be struck dead like—who was it again?

She spent weeks avoiding the book, but the temptation remained too great. A month later, she once again found herself back, enjoying its starchy texture and musty scent.

When she browsed the other parts of the book, she found strange biblical imagery, similar to the seraphim and cherubim she had once seen in an antique illustrated Bible. There was an entire section dedicated to Judaism, with the Ark of the Covenant, Solomon's Temple, and the Second Temple. Hannah marveled at the cherubim, intrigued by their wings and terrified of the eyes that spotted the creature.

> *Following the Israelite Captivity of Babylon, the destruction of Solomon's temple required another location of worship for the reunited Jews. The Second Temple was built following the return from Babylon (now Persia), lasting centuries until its ultimate destruction by the Roman Empire in 70 A.D.*
>
> *The Second Temple had the Parochet Curtain, which separated the Holy of Holies and the Less Holy Place. The Holy of Holies was considered the most sacred ground, the only place where the holy Presence of God could stand to reside. The High Priest was allowed once a year during Yom Kippur, the Day of Atonement in the Holy of Holies, following a specified amount of animal sacrifices.*
>
> *The ordinary Jewish citizen, however, was unable to meet Shekhinah, God's Presence. He was too omnipotent and unreachable, and could only be mentioned through abstract, hushed references.*

Hannah was inexplicably drawn to the visual portrayals of the veil separating the Holy of Holies. The beauties of the interwoven blues and purples! The images of the little cherubim! Behind the veil lay the *Shekhinah*, the Presence of God, something so powerful and uncontained that a veil was needed to conceal the sacred enclosure. Hannah held her breath in awe.

As the girl's hands skimmed through the mysterious book, a haunting melody danced through her mind.

Dancing across, darkness ebbs in, pulsing out as I call to you, waiting…

As the library closed and the night beckoned her, the girl would regretfully leave and plod home to her rotting house with its overgrown grass, blotches of paint, and chipping exterior. Being careful to avoid the shards of glass and cigarette butts scattered on the lawn, Hannah silently unlocked the creaky door and tiptoed to her room. Her father, as usual, was passed out on the couch.

Hannah wondered if it had always been like this. Her earliest memories seemed to be happy, but what changed?

How can I make my mother happy again?

Once during a fight between her parents, Hannah remembered her mom screaming, "If it weren't for my promise, I would have left you long ago!" Hours later, as the daughter helped her mother apply bandages, she asked, "What promise did you make, Mom?"

Her mother wouldn't look her in the eye. "Nothing, Hannah. Nothing."

Although her parents refused to tell her why they fought, Hannah observed her mother, who would experience horrific migraines that prevented her from obtaining a job. She would see her consistently whisper prayers while tears silently streamed down her cheeks, forehead creased in pain.

Years prior, while digging through her mother's room in boredom, Hannah had found a wrinkled document. On it was a large, unfamiliar word:

POSTPARTUM DIAGNOSIS.

During her early elementary school years, Hannah seemed to find herself spending most weekday afternoons in the houses of her classmates and friends, their parents abnormally focused on her. During that time, the girl didn't understand the feeling of pity. However, she did have a notion that her life was not so normal, that there was something different with her family.

Her father seemed to always work late hours. Besides the unpaid bills piling on the kitchen table, he appeared to use his paycheck for drinking a strong, foul liquid, which Hannah later learned was *alcohol*.

Each time Hannah would gather and dispose of the empty bottles, more would appear. Eventually, the daughter stopped attempting to quell the flow of broken glass, instead side-stepping the carnage.

Still, her mother remained highly religious, and the mother and daughter would walk to the nearby church every Sunday morning. Her mother would put on her only nice dress, faded blue with white flowers and a cinched waist. Hannah would wear her pink skirt, which hung to her ankles and sometimes grazed the grass. Although her father would join on special occasions, it was typically the mother and daughter. Her mother was unable to drive, so Hannah would accompany her as they walked, holding her hand and stepping alongside her feeble frame.

Each Sunday, as Hannah listened to the pastor drone on and on, her mother would sway back and forth, whispering and muttering unintelligible prayers. Although Hannah was used to the quiet ramblings and behavior of her mom, her friends would glance at the pair in fear. Their pew frequently remained empty.

As Hannah grew older, she noticed her friends distancing themselves from her, often making excuses about hangouts and not including her in sleepovers and birthday parties. When she asked why, a friend blurted:

"It's because of your parents! My mom thinks your mom is crazy. I'm sorry, Hannah, but I'm not allowed to be your friend anymore."

After that, Hannah spent her days in the library.

As Hannah continued to rock and mutter the melody, she remembered what led to the argument that night:

A year prior, Hannah had discovered a letter addressed to her father. Upon opening it in curiosity, she discovered confessions of love and plans of elopement from a stranger.

The weeks brought a continued stream of love letters, all from different women. Hannah was terrified, afraid to confront her dad yet unable to confide in her bedridden mother, who was spending her days moaning in the damp and moldy bedroom.

That afternoon, her father had driven a moving truck to their house and begun to haul the remaining family heirlooms and valuables away. Hannah had sobbed and begged her father not to leave, to no avail. Her mother, upon discovering divorce papers, collapsed and could not be roused.

As the truck screeched away and her mother began to smash objects, screaming in guttural pain, Hannah ran to her room and slammed the door, crawling under her bed. She rocked back and forth. Back and forth. Back and forth.

Dancing across, darkness ebbs in, pulsing out as I call to you, waiting...

As she shook in fear, Hannah silently pleaded with the God mentioned in her Church's Sunday sermons. A single tear slid down her cheek.

God, where are you? Why are you doing this to me? Why can't I feel you? Please help me. Help me. Please. I'll do anything you want me to do. Just let me know what I can do.

She rocked back and forth, hoping for a reply, until her breathing steadied.

The next morning, Hannah groggily awakened on the gritty bedroom floor. As the memories of the prior day's events returned, she scrambled to her knees. The news of her parents' divorce did not surprise her, and the hollow pit in her stomach had been long suspecting the inevitable.

Suddenly, the girl felt a feeling of dread encompass her. Something was terribly wrong. Where was her mother? The house was eerily quiet, and Hannah could hear a faint creaking noise downstairs.

"Mother? Mother, where are you?" The dread had evolved into a fearful panic, spreading into her body as her heart thumped.

"Mother?"

And as Hannah rounded the bottom of the creaky stairs, she saw the body of her mother hanging limply from the ceiling fan, a rope taut across her neck.

Chapter Five:
Antics of the Unfortunate, A.D. 2540

"Religion is the sigh of the oppressed creature, the heart of a heartless world, and the soul of soulless conditions. It is the opium of the people."

—Karl Marx,
A Contribution to the Critique of Hegel's Philosophy of Right

A.D. 2540 – Former Chicago; Glacier National Park, USA

Snake! The boy backed away in fear, eyes glazed in terror. A stone's throw away from him was a large, coiled snake with red eyes. Staring right at him, its cold eyes seemed to probe into the child's soul like a cold breeze, freezing everything in its path. "Stay away from me!" he screamed. "Leave me alone!"

Heart pumping in fear, the boy whipped around and fled out of the forest, barging his way through the brush. When he finally reached the wastelands of rotting steel frames and debris, the child lay down, catching his breath and steadying his nerves. There was something strange about the snake. Although he had been terrified of snakes all his life, it seemed as though this particular creature was always following him.

He gingerly side-stepped the wastelands, attempting to avoid the debris remaining from the vagabonds who frequently prowled the ruins. Outside the rotting building structures, railroad skeleton, and ugly remainders of statues, the landscape sported few hopes for food or shelter. Raids on camps tended to be much more successful.

His rag-tag group, composed mostly of older men, had told him the city used to be called *Chicago*. "What a strange name," he had remarked.

"Everything used to be strange," a limping older man rebutted. "That's why the world ended."

Nobody in the group had names. The boy instead characterized them by their features. One man had lost his right arm when a buried explosive detonated. Another sported a noticeable limp. Still another had sandy-blond hair that tended to cover his sky-blue eyes.

And then there was his mother. The teenager had never known life without Tamar, who was completely deaf. She used to sing to him when he was younger before an illness wiped out her hearing, almost taking her life away as well.

Dancing across, darkness ebbs in, pulsing out as I call to you, waiting...

"Where did you learn that song, Mom?" The boy was

fascinated by the eerie melody, not understanding the meaning of the song or its rather dark implications.

"My family used to live on a remote farm many years ago, when I was around your age. Growing up, my mother would tell me and my siblings the story about how our ancestors survived and fled with their books when the world was ending. They told me how they found the farm after the nuclear war. One day, a raid killed my parents and took me. I was a slave for years, but I managed to run away. After months of wandering the forests, I was certain that I was going to die, just like the rest of my family. But one night, I saw a woman with coal-black eyes beckoning me, singing this melody. I followed her voice until I was led outside the forest and into a beautiful meadow with a stream and wild berries. That was where I raised you, do you remember?"

The child peered into his mother's intense green eyes as she tousled his sandy-brown hair. He reminisced about fading memories in a sunny meadow, roasted hares that his mother caught with traps, and the lush grass that he used to frolic in. His mother named him Hare, since the duo survived on wild hares that frequented the plains. Ever since his mother lost her hearing, she was mute, making indistinguishable noises instead of words. But she would still recognize when Hare would sing her melody.

Dancing across, darkness ebbs in, pulsing out as I call to you, waiting...

Over a decade prior, when Hare's mom fled into the forests during the dead of night, she was violated, malnourished, and covered in bruises. During her months wandering in the wilderness, the young woman realized she was pregnant. Initial horror and fear soon evolved into motherly preservation, a determination to save the life of her child, who was beginning to kick in her womb.

When Tamar was led by the mysterious woman into the meadow, the young woman was heavily pregnant and beginning to experience labor pains. Although she survived on catching fish and foraging for wild berries, the woman took her across an abandoned hunting lodge with hunting snares and bows, which the woman used to capture the wild hares and squirrels that frequented the paths, sustaining the remainder of her final trimester.

The night Hare was born, there was a horrific rainstorm. Flashes of lightning branded the pitch-black night, illuminating the sky, and periodically, a bolt would strike a tree, lighting the sizzled trunk into flames. Tamar had crawled into her makeshift enclosure after her water broke: a large tree which had collapsed long ago into a boulder, insulated by a bed of mulch, leaves, and soft grasses. The labor lasted the entire night, accompanied by the cacophony of thunder, pouring rain, and the theatrics of horrific flashes of lightning.

Tamar placed a dense maple branch between her teeth as her face contorted in pain. Her mouth began to bleed from the sharp shards that burrowed into her mouth wall. The stick, dyed red, splintered from the exertion. Then, it snapped.

The Curtain Between Us

Yet still, her child was stuck. The laboring mother was rapidly losing her energy. Covered in sweat and screaming in pain, Tamar dug her nails into the bloodied earth and wailed.

A bolt of lightning illuminated a nearby tree. The woman seemed motionless. And there was a figure approaching.

Tamar had never believed in a higher power. As she had told Hare, if a God existed, he seemed to delight only in inflicting torment and pain. "What did I ever do to deserve it?" she asked. "What does anyone do to deserve the hellhole we're stuck in? We can't even leave, and if we decide to take the easy way out, we're damned for eternity."

Her parents had taught her how to read as they were taught by their parents, and before their farm was discovered and raided, she would read ancient classics and ponderings of tortured individuals doubting the existence of a loving Creator. She learned about the religious wars in the Medieval Ages, the Crusades, Islamic jihadism, and the massacres conducted in the name of God. "Remember this," her parents told her. "Although most of society is wiped out, books never die. Their ideas live forever through the minds of those who remember."

Tamar herself concluded that religion, just like any other ideology, was only created by the authorities to maintain their power and quell their subjects into obedience and civil behavior. Nothing, after all, is more powerful than convincing the masses of an afterlife in damnation.

"Life is difficult," her parents explained. "But we will never run away from that. However, beware of religion and her lies. A good God would never do this to his people. Everyone who believes so is foolish, lying to themselves so that they don't face the reality of the universe's suffering." Closing her eyes, lashes fluttering, Tamar remembered the story of Iphis, the unfortunate daughter of Jephthah. She was the only child of the prophet and was burned in fire for his rash vow. A daughter condemned to death through the words of her own father.

"Why," Tamar asked, "did Iphis have to die? What did she do to deserve that? Why was she condemned to burn?"

Her questioning was always met by silence.

The day the farm was raided, Tamar's younger sister had spotted a group of vagabonds in the distance. They were approaching quickly and appeared to be carrying torches. Her siblings were ordered to hide the valuables and the books, concealing them in a cave by the farm. Tamar, her siblings, and the women hid in the loft while the men gathered weapons crafted by their family and prepared for confrontation.

Although Tamar and her siblings would occasionally sight traveling groups of vagabonds, a warning shot had always served as a deterrent. Only loners, the sick, and the pregnant were allowed entry and medical attention. That was how Tamar's father had entered the farm and married her mother. Her father was a part of another isolated commune that had been attacked and raided by vagabonds and had fled and lived as a recluse until discovering the farm and marrying Tamar's mother. But he was an exception.

"Do not ever trust strangers," her mother would tell the children. "Especially groups of men. They are dead souls that prowl in the shadows, hoping to siphon life and warmth from the living. Once they ensnare you, your body becomes an eternal vessel for their pleasures." Tamar quivered in fear. One of her sisters started crying. "Tamar," her mother whispered gently. "Promise me. Never let yourself be taken by men. Tell me you would rather die than allow yourself to be captured by them."

The girl's soft green eyes locked with watery ones full of sadness. "Yes, Mama.

"I promise."

As the vagabonds drew closer, Tamar saw a large group of over fifty men—far outnumbering the family. They had only five men, with ten women, children, and elders hiding in the loft. "Help us," the girl heard her mother whisper. She clung to her sisters and cried.

They are dead souls that prowl in the shadows, hoping to siphon life and warmth from the living.

What happened next was mostly blocked by the girl after decades of suppression and denial. When straining to remember, Tamar would recall the sound of bodies clashing against each other, metal hitting metal, then gunfire. She remembered sharp shouts of agony and the rattles of death, but she was unable to distinguish who made those noises. Her memories omitted the eventual stillness, silent weeping from her family members in the attic, and sharp curses and the cracks of bursting barrels as the vagabonds were unable to discover any valuables other than food.

Their voices held deep anger and something far more sinister.

Once they ensnare you, your body becomes an eternal vessel for their pleasures.

However, one scene, decades later, would remain seared into her mind.

Tamar remembered the locked attic door being kicked open: the frame splitting, the pain of stinging shards making impact with soft skin. And she remembered the hardened, bloodshot eyes of the vagabonds.

Upon forced entry, the men were first greeted by a girl with wild green eyes.

Promise me. Never let yourself be taken by men. Tell me you would rather die than allow yourself to be captured by them.

Cries of fear erupted from the women alongside screams from Tamar and her siblings and surprised grunts from the old men. Like cattle, the women were rounded up together while the children were forcibly dragged away by the men. *Mother! Where is she?* Tamar sank her teeth into her captor's fleshy hand. With a sickening snap of crushed bones, the metallic taste of warm blood entered her mouth. The man screamed in agony, alerting the other vagabonds.

A wave of searing heat slammed into the girl as she was pummeled by the men. She tried to scream, but blood dribbled out. In rage, the injured man kicked her in the head, turning her world black. She crumpled, lifeless, into a pool of blood.

Tamar didn't hear her mother's hysterical cries, her siblings screaming her name over and over. It was the last time she would ever see her family.

As her vision blurred, the young girl remembered why Iphis was condemned to burn.

She was the first living being her father laid his eyes on, celebrating his victory.

Like Iphis, Tamar now knew the cost of being the first one seen.

As Tamar's limp body was dragged out of the compound where she had spent her whole life, slumped corpses and carnage lay in her wake. Silenced screams and gunshots from the attic confirmed the fate of her remaining relatives.

The men split up, and Tamar was dragged into the forest, marking an exodus from her former life.

Yes, Mama. I promise.

These memories all resurfaced in Tamar's mind as she breathed agonizingly, her body being ripped open from the inside. Her son was stuck, and she was alone in the rain, preparing for their demise. Her vision began to blur at the edges, and her pushes became weaker and less frequent. *Help me,* she thought weakly. *If you're out there, please help me.*

As her breaths began to slow, Tamar became aware of a presence beside her, guiding her. *I'm here,* the mysterious woman whispered. *You'll be alright.* Tamar felt the woman's soft touch guiding and adjusting her child out, guiding her own breathing, singing to her. Her long black hair flowed over Tamar, and her touch felt like the cold pricks of wooden splinters.

Dancing across, darkness ebbs in, pulsing out as I call to you, waiting...

In one final push, her child came out, the sound of rain interrupted by sharp cries. "Thank you," Tamar whispered, "I don't even know who you are." The woman embraced the mother one last time. "Your son will do great things, but he will shatter your heart," she murmured. Stroking her head gently, the spirit breathed, "Remember one thing: he will crush your head, and you will strike his heel." Without a trace, she then vanished into the storm.

Hare heard the story of his birth from his mother many times, and as the years passed, he began to hum and sing the tune as he skipped across the streams and scaled the trees. His mother, however, never told him the prophecies breathed over him that night.

Dancing across, darkness ebbs in, pulsing out as I call to you, waiting...

As Hare grew into adolescence, his increased height and muscular frame enabled him to fiercely protect his mother. The animals in the clearing were peaceful and reclusive, but snakes had always terrified him. In his nightmares, there would be a snake coiled around him, its red eyes boring into his soul.

One morning, as Hare was helping his mother across an unfamiliar stream to pick berries, a stone she stepped on exploded.

Instantly, both were thrown across the riverbank as the eruption launched Tamar into a nearby cliff overhang. *That's not a stone. It's a bomb from the war.* Hare's vision blurred with pain, then darkened.

As he woke up, head pounding, Hare struggled to stand up. *Where's my mother?* Whipping his head around, he found Tamar barely breathing and unconscious at the foot of the cliff. Blood pooled around her lifeless body. The young man cried in fear, scooping his mother up and rushing back to the enclave. Although he attempted to bandage her bleeding with moss, Hare could understand the situation. His mother, although awake now, was unable to speak or hear. Her wound, although temporarily closed, would sporadically burst. Tamar spent the days drifting in and out of consciousness, unable to eat. Her eyes began to glaze over.

One day, burning with fever, the woman began to thrash. Hare decided to act, making a journey past everything he had known. Carrying his frail mother, he headed into the forest, toward the vagabond dwellings. As he walked past the familiar wooded areas and streams, trails and overhangs, Hare continued to follow the mental instructions given by a vagabond years prior. "A large group of us lives on the outskirts of a former city—Chicago, I think. We're friendly and we don't kill. We survive by hunting and plundering food from other groups. I think you should join. If you follow the North Star, you'll find an old truck yard, which was used by the previous people. You'll see the remnants of the train tracks, which you will follow until a clearing by the lake. When asked, tell them you're a moon-tracker."

When the boy gave him a confused glance, the vagabond shrugged. "That's the code we decided on."

As the boy plodded through the train tracks, reassuring his half-conscious mother, he saw the outlines of a lake and shadowy figures. "Help!" he screamed. "Moon-tracker! Moon-tracker!"

Mother, you will never die when I am here. I will protect you. You gave me life. I will keep you alive.

"We're here!" Hare yelled. "We're moon-trackers! My mother is dying!" As shouts sounded, Hare breathed a sigh of relief.

"Mother," he whispered. "Help is coming."

He collapsed to the ground.

Chapter Six:
Rituals and the Like, A.D. 2552

"Each lost soul will be a hell unto itself, the boundless fire raging in its very vitals."

—James Joyce,
A Portrait of the Artist as a Young Man

A.D. 2552 – Former Pikes Peak, Rocky Mountains

Hagar exhaled a sigh of boredom as Mrs. Elise, her stuffy schoolteacher, droned on and on. She was now old enough to join the school system, where she would be expected to learn basic arithmetic, reading, and writing from the Bible. Mrs. Elise had been the schoolteacher for over twenty years now. *Twenty years too long*, Hagar thought bitterly.

The Remnant originally had a few copies of the Bible saved by the original settlers, who had fled with their prized possessions. Those Bibles were kept in safety by the Elders, and only they could read and handle them. The ones the settlers held were copies of those original Bibles, painstakingly inscribed by quills by appointed scribes. These scribes were chosen by the Elders and dedicated their lives to inscribing the Word. When a husband and wife got married in front of the Curtain, they would be gifted a precious Bible from the Elders. It was said that the book was a foundation for the new family, words and stories that the following generation would be raised on.

But for the schoolhouse, there was a tattered picture book and a copy for the teacher, Mrs. Elise.

In addition to academic learning, there were also lectures on the structure and history of the Remnant, and the roles that would be expected of the children once they become adults.

"The Remnant," Hagar's schoolteacher droned, "was established sometime in the 2100s following the destruction of the previous world in the nuclear war. There were two world wars prior to that, but the nuclear war was the third and final. Nobody knew which country dropped the first nuclear bomb, because right after, all the countries that possessed nuclear weapons dropped them on their opponents, targeting major cities and populated hubs."

"The bloodshed was massive, and it is assumed that the majority of the world was lost within days. Over the months and years after, most of the survivors perished from famine, murder, and looting. The few buildings that remained standing were completely ransacked. As for modern machinery—you have never heard about airplanes, vehicles, and trucks. Those are large objects that people once climbed into that allowed them to fly like birds and run faster than deer in the forest. These were all destroyed, too.

"It is important to realize that the story of Eve," Mrs. Elise continued, "can be learned from the previous society's collapse. Just like Eve fell to the serpent's deceit and led her husband to sin, women led the flourishing of the previous civilization, often choosing the world over their duties as women. Their selfishness and straying from their biblical duties contributed to the Fall.

"Our ancestors survived because they lived in communities away from the sinful cities. Although many died from radioactive poisoning after bombs were dropped, some survived and fled with their families and possessions into the wilderness. As the vagabonds began to loot and murder the surviving settlers, the community of pious religious survivors ventured into the East, avoiding any sign of human life and surviving through hunting animals and foraging.

"As members began to perish and disappear in the unforgiving wilderness through disease, injuries, animal attacks, and occasional raids, the group was broken and convinced that God had abandoned the world and turned his back upon the people. During this difficult period, the Elders gathered in deep prayer and revealed that the adolescents in the group were called to wander in the wilderness until the Spirit came upon them. When they were filled with the Spirit, God would have mercy on them.

"That night, over five hundred years ago, five unnamed

teenagers were chosen by the Elders. The community prayed over them and blessed them before sending them into the wilderness as an offering to their God, an attempt to appease the Divine who had seemingly abandoned them.

"A week passed, and there was no sign of them. The community became listless and agitated; some wicked men and women even suggested leaving the group! However, on the eve of the seventh day, one member came back, filled with the Spirit and noticeably changed. He claimed that while he was in deep prayer and fasting, God revealed that he was to lead the group toward their new home.

"The next day, the two girls returned. The Spirit was upon them, and they seemed to glow with an iridescent light. They were speaking in tongues, praising the Lord and describing their new home.

"On the morning of the ninth day, one of the remaining boys returned. He was dancing with joy and announced to the community that God had provided him the direction to their final home. Late that evening, the last boy returned. He claimed to have received sights of a new food source, but his demeanor was peculiar, and when other community members followed him to the suspected place, there was nothing. Under pressure from the Elders, the boy admitted that he had not received anything from the Lord and, in the moment, had decided to create a false narrative.

"After a meeting held by the Elders, they determined that the boy must be cast out as he had endangered the community through his deceit and did not receive God's favor. After asking God to have mercy on the cursed teenager, they drove him out.

"The four teenagers who received God's Spirit were chosen to be the first anointed adults, having successfully received the grace of God. They led the community to the Curtain and the lush meadows nearby. They were anointed mature members of the congregation under the Curtain, and the Elders of the community matched the two women and men as husband and wife.

"The pious example of the four teenagers became the model for the generations to come. When you finish school after eight years, the Elders will determine if you are ready to go through your mission and receive the Spirit. If not, you will be held back until they determine your eligibility. Once you're ready, the Elders will have a conversation with you inside the Abode, a sacred spot in the forest where the Elders meet to worship. Some years, adolescents have been sent out in groups, although they are commanded to spend their time in complete isolation. Other years, only one adolescent was deemed eligible. The community prays over the chosen and they are sent out, ordered not to return until they receive the Presence."

"But Mrs. Elise," Abigail whispered, "what if a person never receives it?"

The schoolteacher shook her head in disappointment. "That is extremely rare," she said slowly. "But it has happened before. The Elders have made it clear that if the Lord does not show favor, the person is not to come back."

Some of the girls, who sat at the left side of the classroom, gasped while the boys, who sat at the right-hand side, shifted nervously. Abigail cried, her soft eyes stricken with terror.

"If the adolescent does not return for over a month, they are assumed to be damned and their identity is erased. They may have died in the forests, or they just never received the Presence. There have been a few examples where a prospect returns but is determined not to have received the Spirit. On such cases, the Elders gather to determine their fate. Some are driven out into the forest, where they are to be shot on sight. Others are pushed off the cliff."

At this point, Hagar's hands began to quiver. Hagar had not told anyone about her inability to feel the Presence. She couldn't help glancing at her sister Abigail, whose eyes had widened at the mention of the cliff. Yes, Hagar would not tell anyone her secret, not even Abigail, much less her father or other sisters. But the terror that she would be found out always lingered.

At this thought, her head began to throb, something which had been occurring more frequently the past few weeks. Ever since Hagar was a child, she had struggled with debilitating headaches, where it felt like her brain was squeezed like a rag getting wrung of water. Often, the girl would find a dark spot in the cellar and rock back and forth, crying as she lay in a fetal position. *Jesus, Son of David, have mercy on me. Jesus, Son of David, have mercy on me. Help me, help me, help me.* Tears streamed down her cheeks, dropping onto the dusty floor. *Help me.*

The Curtain Between Us

As Hagar's thoughts drifted back to her class, she realized that Mrs. Elise had returned to lecturing: "This practice," she remarked, "has led to a flourishing community blessed by his Presence. Following their return, adolescents every year are appointed as adults, blessed into arranged marriages, and assigned occupations by the Elders to bless the Remnant. After your marriage, you are given your own Bible and encouraged to be fruitful and multiply."

With the conclusion of the sentence, the bell for prayer rang. "Well," Mrs. Elise chirped. "Time for prayer."

Prayer was once a day in the afternoon, and the entire village was mandated to attend. Unless someone was on their deathbed or in labor, failure to attend could be reported and lead to expulsion by the Elders.

As Hagar joined her friends, bouncing together and giggling about the boys, the words still rattled in her chest, heavy as stones.

What if I become one of those damned? What if I never feel anything? Would it be possible to fake it?

She shook her head in impatience. Now was not the time.

As the group approached the rock outcropping, girls gathering in their spots to the left and the boys to the right, Hagar saw the women ahead of them and the men in the front. As the community began to pray and chant for mercy, Hagar flatly whispered the same prayers.

Help me, God. Help me.

Her friends began to sway and chant in tongues, and

Hagar tried to emulate them.

God, make me like them. I want to be like them. I want to feel you.

The wind whistled across the clearing, and Hagar aimlessly watched a leaf glide across the stone and fall into the abyss.

Chapter Seven:
The Pain of Living, A.D. 1995

"But a caged bird stands on the grave of dreams / his shadow shouts on a nightmare scream / his wings are clipped and his feet are tied / so he opens his throat to sing."
—Maya Angelou, "Caged Bird"

A.D. 1995 – Minneapolis, USA

Hannah rocked back and forth, her eyes glazed and vacant. It had been five years since she discovered her mother's lifeless body hanging from the ceiling fan, but the bulging eyes, purple face, and continuous creaking from the corpse held taut by the swinging rope still appear in her nightmares. Night after night, paralyzed with dread, Hannah would desperately attempt to claw herself out of her torment.

But she never could. The cruelties of her memory wouldn't allow for that. It would be too kind.

Hannah still relived her horrified screams, the smell and look of death, the blaring sirens, and the eventual silence. She has been in and out of foster homes for five years, hospitalized numerous times, injected with sedatives until the pain faded into nothingness.

She had attempted, twice. The first time, she swallowed a vial of antidepressants, only to wake up puking uncontrollably, a searing pain spreading in her body. She never told anyone.

The second time, like her mother, Hannah had attempted to hang herself. The fan in her middle school storage area broke, sending the girl tumbling to the ground. When the janitor opened the door, confused about the commotion, he found a trembling teenager with a rope around her neck next to a broken fan, face streaked with tears, face bleeding and streaked with tears.

After a lengthy hospitalization, Hannah had been put on powerful medications.

But still, as the seventeen-year-old returned to her disheveled bed and stared at the popcorn ceiling, tears flowed silently amidst muffled sobs. Despite whispered pleas for her sleeping meds to kick in, her misery returned, slamming into her like a brick wall.

Dancing across, darkness ebbs in, pulsing out as I call to you, waiting...

The song, which Hannah heard five years prior, began to reappear. Uninterested, she shoved the melody aside.

As she lay awake, thoughts paralyzed by depression,

Hannah remembered that she would be eighteen tomorrow. The past years bouncing between foster homes were miserable, with each of her foster parents initially attempting to connect with the girl but eventually giving up. She was a lost cause, an irreparably damaged soul.

However, when she turned eighteen, Hannah was aware of her fate: being left to fend for herself, to manage her own finances and living expenses, to find a job and maybe go to college. She was not ready, not when she spent half the day sobbing in her bed. Her schoolwork was a hopeless cause as well. She had neither the finances nor the willpower to attend college.

What would she do? Hannah toyed around with the idea of following in her mother's footsteps. Her father had no interest in her besides paying for minimal child support fees, which would end once she came of age. Her grandparents had never been in the picture. She had no friends and spent the school day napping or staring at the ceiling. She had no one to love. She should just...

No. She was too cowardly. It was too much effort to buy rope, tie it to the ceiling, and put the noose around her neck when she couldn't even muster the energy to adjust her position in bed.

Tomorrow, the girl would be considered a legal adult. She would age out of the foster system. She would need to find a job and get her own apartment. The thought kept the girl wide awake.

Shaking her head in frustration, Hannah tumbled out of

bed and rummaged through her possessions. There was something she wanted to read. Sifting through, she found it: a folded, yellowed letter addressed to her. Blinking, Hannah sat down and reopened it.

> *My dearest Hannah,*
>
> *Your mother is writing this letter to you for you to read when you're older.*
>
> *I am feeling your kicks right now, and they bring me and your father endless joy! We have prayed for you for years. I was diagnosed as infertile by my doctors, and my heart was broken. I always wanted to have a child, and you became the answer to our prayers.*
>
> *When I prayed to God for a child, I told him I was willing to sacrifice anything. After I became pregnant, I felt God tell me that he has great plans for you, that you will inspire many people in the centuries following. That brought me so much hope.*
>
> *God told me that I would be making a great sacrifice, but I believe that you are the light to our family, a miracle baby.*
>
> *With great anticipation,*
>
> *Your Mother.*

Wiping the tears from her face, Hannah whispered the word.

Postpartum.

Her mother's pregnancy had wreaked havoc on her body, and the woman never fully recovered. During the third trimester, the doctors realized that Hannah posed a serious health risk to her mother and strongly recommended an abortion.

It was likely that Hannah's birth would be extremely difficult, and there was a chance that her mother would die during labor. Nonetheless, her parents persisted. Their dreams for a child had been answered, and they would not give up easily.

As the day of her delivery came closer, Hannah's mother was unable to eat without puking, and her body shriveled under the duress. After her water broke, she was in labor for two days, screaming as Hannah refused to come out. After an emergency C-section, Hannah's mother went into a coma and lost much of her blood.

But they had a daughter.

After she woke up, Hannah's mother went into a deep postpartum depression. She refused medications and would spend days shut in a dark room, ignoring pleas from her husband.

Hannah's father was forced to do all the housework while working a full-time job, as well as taking care of Hannah and her depressed mother. Years of this took a toll on the man, and he soon turned to alcohol and prostitutes to cope.

By the time he filed for divorce, the man was utterly

exhausted, struggling with liver problems, and done with married life. As far as Hannah was aware, he spent his life savings in Las Vegas, gambling after work. Her father didn't even bother to attend his late wife's funeral, simply placing his daughter in foster care before disappearing with his current mistress.

Maybe he married his lover. Maybe they had children.

As Hannah read through the letter, she remembered that she was the reason for her parents' divorce, her mother's suicide, her father's misery. If she had never been born, her parents would probably still be married and happy together.

If only her parents had never prayed for her.

No, she thought. *It's a lie.* Hope was a knife, a deceptive object that only brought pain and agony. She wasn't sure she could survive another cut on her own.

The clock struck twelve.

Hannah was eighteen.

Chapter Eight:
Tragedy in Mizpah, 982 B.C.

"Then the Spirit of the LORD came on Jephthah. He crossed Gilead and Manasseh, passed through Mizpah of Gilead, and from there he advanced against the Ammonites. And Jephthah made a vow to the LORD: "If you give the Ammonites into my hands, whatever comes out of the door of my house to meet me when I return in triumph from the Ammonites will be the LORD's, and I will sacrifice it as a burnt offering."
—Judges 11:29–31 (NIV)

982 B.C. – Mizpah, Ancient Israel

Iphis, Iphis! A swarm of children pranced around the young woman, whose curly locks bounced as she sang the Song of Miriam:

"Sing to the Lord,
for he has triumphed gloriously!
The horse and its rider
he has thrown into the sea!"

Iphis smiled at the squealing children, who were fighting for an opportunity to fly, suspended in the breeze, by their favorite person. "Jacoub," she called, "you're next." She hoisted the boy up and began to spin around, making her circles tighter and faster. Jacoub yelped in delight, his chubby legs kicking in the air.

After a few rotations, the landscape and trees blurred together, a palette of colors swirled into a mixture by a brush. Staggering, Iphis set the boy down, making sure not to land on any children as she dropped to the ground. The courtyard again erupted in joyful squeals.

"Alright, alright, get off her!" Iphis breathed a relieved sigh as the groaning boys and girls reluctantly trotted away. "תודה לך" she breathed in gratitude to the older women, who whisked the children to another courtyard. *Toda lech.*

Her father, Jephthah the Gileadite, was a mighty warrior in Israel and had recently defeated the Ammonites, horrific pagans who committed every abominable sin under the sun. Adonai be praised, the Israelites had purged the land of those evils. And the men were due to return today!

Iphis smiled at the thought of her father. She was his only child, born after many years of infertility. Her mother had died in labor. But to her father, grief was replaced by fierce defense of his daughter.

Every year, on the tenth day of the seventh month, Iphis would go to Yom Kippur with her father to make atonement. They would bring two of their flock's best goats and a prized ram for the yearly sin offering and burnt offering. Each year, Iphis would help her father choose the offerings to Adonai. However, each time she would avert her gaze, shuddering as the knife was plunged into the animal's throat. As life drained from their eyes, a tear slid down her cheek.

The father, a warrior of Israel and hardened by the years of battle, softened as he saw his daughter distraught at the brutal reality of living. She couldn't understand death or the meaning of rituals.

"My daughter," Jephthah soothed. "We obey, because Adonai sees what we cannot. What we do is obey."

"What we do is obey," Iphis repeated softly. She glanced back once more at the Holy City, the dwelling place of God.

Iphis blinked, rubbing her face. It was time to slaughter the prized calf. The animal had been fattened its entire existence for an occasion like this. She breathed deeply, preparing for the inevitable, before following the village men to the enclosure.

As they surrounded the calf, the animal began to snort and trot nervously around. Iphis's heart beat rapidly, pounding against her chest.

She stepped into the enclosure.

The animal gazed at her.

"There's nothing to fear, my darling." Iphis had raised the calf since their cow, his mother, died months ago.

The animal trotted over, eager to see his owner again.

Running her fingers across his body and scratching the itchy parts behind his ears, Iphis whispered reassurances to her friend. She then sang a lullaby to the calf, guiding it down to the ground while stroking the creature's coat. A tear rolled down her cheek as her heart twisted.

Hush, my darling, as you lay on the ground. I sing this lullaby to you. As you follow the paths trodden before, you follow the ancestors into the great unknown. Praise Adonai, he has chosen you for his praise. May the Almighty have mercy on your soul.

The animal looked at Iphis, eyes unsearchable. Iphis silently beckoned the men over, still whispering reassurances to her calf.

"May the Almighty have mercy on your soul." With that, the butcher sliced through the windpipe of the animal. The animal exhaled, blood streaming out of the wound. His eyes emptied and went cold.

Iphis felt a chill run through her spine.

What have I done?

As the preparations finished and the calf was roasting over the fire, Iphis heard the distant plods of marching.

"The men are back!" she joyfully sang, grabbing a timbrel and giving some to her servants. The children, fueled by her excitement, clamored with her. "The men are back!" they sang. "Praise Adonai!"

As Iphis skipped forward, an elder gently grasped her shoulder, brows furrowed in dread. "My child," he said, "I have a strange feeling. I think you should stay back."

Iphis smiled gently, shaking her head. Giving the elder an apologetic glance, she rushed toward the paths, the children running beside her. As her feet glided down the road, Iphis strained her eyes, seeing the encroaching mass of men in the distance. Her father, she knew, would be at the front.

Iphis quickened, feet pattering and arms pumped out. *Father, I'm coming.* After what seemed like an eternity, she saw the face of her father.

"Father!" she yelled hoarsely. The children, some shaking the timbrels and singing, were still in the distance.

At the sight of his daughter, Jephthah cried in dismay, dropping his sword and falling to the ground.

"Adonai," he cried. "What have I done?"

Iphis knew her fate was unavoidable. Her father had made a rash vow to Adonai, vowing that the first to greet him would be sacrificed as an offering if the Israelites were victorious. Intending to meet an unsuspecting servant, he had instead stumbled across his only child.

She had firmly reassured her father, knowing that a vow given to Adonai could never be taken back. There was nothing she could do.

Iphis requested two months to wander the mountains of Manasseh, precious time to reconcile with her impending death and the loss of her future. She would never be betrothed, never have the opportunity to make love to a man or bear his children. Instead, she was to be burned alive on a stake. Hopefully she would suffocate from the fumes before she felt the flames eat her alive.

One night, as she pleaded in distress to the distant Almighty, Iphis felt the dread of her situation replace itself with intense fear. "Lord," she cried. "Why are you doing this to me?"

The stars continued to shine. There was no response, no burning bush like Moses, no intervening vision like her forefather Ibrahim.

She was met with the sound of deafening silence.

Weeping and shaking uncontrollably, Iphis remembered the words of her father, years prior:

"Adonai's ways can never be comprehended. He is higher than we can ever reach, and we can never understand his purpose or motives. What we do is obey." Dread coursed through her body. Above all else, the young girl felt pure, unadulterated terror. She didn't want to die.

"Adonai's ways are higher," she breathed. "The only thing I can do is obey."

Legs quivering, Iphis shuddered violently as the ropes were tied around her. Her head screamed as tremors of terror shot up her body. She felt a warm sensation down her legs. Looking down, she saw a yellow puddle near her feet. She had wet herself.

Around her, the smell of slaughter already thickened the

air. Blood was scattered on the ground from the animal sacrifices earlier in the morning.

The scent of damp stone and cedar overwhelmed her senses. A warm metallic taste filled her mouth. Iphis sputtered. She had drawn blood.

Iphis heard the lapping of flames, which began to consume the wood piled under her. Panic briefly overwhelmed her as the flames began to rise. *I can't die. No! I'm too young! I have never known a man. Where is Father?*

Iphis whipped her head around. Her father was nowhere in sight. The fear turned into anger. "Father!" she screamed. "Father!"

The chants echoed in a haunting rhythm, the drums beating as she began to choke on burning smoke, shuddering uncontrollably. Scorching flames lapped at her feet, the sensation searing like a knife through her body.

The screams that ripped from her body faded into paralyzing numbness. Iphis, consumed by a cloud of thick black smoke, exhaled, the panic coursing through her veins fading as her flesh began to melt.

Iphis closed her eyes and murmured the words her father instilled in her long ago.

"What we do is obey."

"What we do is obey."

Adonai, have mercy on my soul.

Chapter Nine: Mother and Son, A.D. 2552

"The tongue may hide the truth but the eyes—never!"
—Mikhail Bulgakov, *The Master and Margarita*

A.D. 2552 – Rocky Mountains, Former Colorado, USA

Hare narrowed his blue eyes in suspicion as he watched his mother amble across the paths. Every year, the Chicago vagabonds would go on a raid, and this year was no different. Hare, although never fond of raiding communities, felt obligated to the men.

Tamar never left his sight. Whenever a man would attempt to get too close, Hare would stand between, his eyes boring into the man until he eventually scurried off.

Nobody hurts my mother. No one.

Tamar's recovery had been challenging. Unable to hear or speak, she gradually regained the strength to walk after several months. Though she was never the same—often staring blankly into space, wandering erratically, or conversing with no one in particular—she remained Hare's mother, his anchor. Now, she was in charge of snaring prey and bringing wild produce for their vagabond group. But Hare insisted on accompanying his mother.

As the group crept across the path, Tamar trailing behind, the man with the missing arm stopped briefly. "We're nearing," he whispered. "Listen."

The past few months, the men had heard rumors of an isolated group near the bottom edge of the former Rocky Mountains. It would be impossible to infiltrate the camp before the attack.

Their ragtag group was joined by multiple vagabond units, who were willing to share their resources and plunder. "Just keep heading southwest," they were told. "You'll make contact after a few weeks."

The vagabonds, although vicious, lived by a moral code. They were simply after food and possessions. Although other groups would snatch women and children, the Chicago vagabonds refused to harm human life. No blood was to be spilled.

As they neared the compound, Hare stretched his body. He had grown over the past few months, feeling a constant ravenous hunger and aching joints. Now, he stood above the other vagabonds, and he secretly enjoyed looking at the surface of the water, watching his reflection as his muscles rippled.

He was a man now.

The men stopped and began to climb the trees. Hare nodded to his mother, who stopped and sat on the bumpy floor. As the men looked around, they saw the telltale marker of the commune. There was a large, dark, red and blue object in the distance, something like a curtain. Across the ledge, a sea of people kneeled on the stone, murmuring and crying in unison.

They had reached their target.

"This should be an easy job," said the man with sandy-blond hair, his hands again brushing across his eyes.

"I do wonder," the man with the missing arm murmured, "how they got that darn thing across the cliff."

"Ehh," Hare remarked. "Shh—I see a guard!"

The vagabonds caught a glimpse of a lone man marching across the clearing in circles, a rusty musket slung across his body. Hare noiselessly slid down and moved his mother by a fallen tree trunk, shushing her gently. What a peculiar camp.

For today, the best loot would be weapons, storage packs, and gold. Weapons were always appreciated. The men had a difficult time creating their own packs out of fabric, which limited the amount of supplies they could carry. And gold was a prized item for trade.

The men floated across, making a circle around the unaware guard. Hare grabbed his pocketknife. The man with blond hair carried an old revolver, the limping man wielded a club, and the one-armed man held a steak knife. Among the recent arrivals from the night prior, Hare spotted a bulky man with shaggy brown hair and a torn ear pacing around.

Upon deeper study, he realized half of the man's left ear was ripped off, with dried clumps of blood caked around the shredded cartilage. The healing was uneven, and a flap of hanging skin covered what appeared to be another rip. Something about the man seemed wrong, something sinister about the cold glint in his eyes. His icy blue eyes gleamed with vengeance and something else the boy was unable to decipher.

I'll keep an eye on him, Hare decided. He narrowed his eyes, glaring as their eyes met. *Don't even think about touching my mother.*

Each man sported a bag for placing their possessions as well as a weapon of choice.

"Mother," Hare whispered. "Don't move." He motioned for her to stay and beckoned a fellow man over. "Keep an eye over her," he whispered, "and half of my plunder will be yours."

Behind, the warrior heard a yelp of alarm from the guard, then silence as he was swarmed. The other men, numbering almost fifty, charged the camp. Horns were blasted. A battle cry seared through the bright sky.

Hare sprinted and caught up with the others, all crashing into the village encampment at once. The village was built with small log houses, each one with a small, fenced yard and animals tied to posts. The women, covered in long veils, clung to their children.

Upon hearing the ruckus and seeing the invaders, the villagers shrieked in shock and ran into their houses. The men cast wary glances at each other. *Would they have weapons? Would they fight?*

"We won't hurt you," the men roared. "Just leave your houses."

As the men began barging into the old log homes, kicking the doors down, Hare screamed, "Don't shoot! Don't shoot! Don't hurt them!" The air was filled with screams of fear and angry yells by the raiders, glass shattering and the squeals of livestock.

Please don't fight back, he thought. *I don't want to kill you.*

Kicking a door open to screams, Hare grabbed the family's packs and blankets. He paused briefly as his eyes met a leather-bound book. He couldn't read, but he knew how much his mother loved books.

THE HOLY BIBLE

For a moment, Hare was torn. There were much better things, more useful prizes than an old book. Shrugging in exasperation, he snatched it, ignoring the cries of the woman hiding in the corner.

As he emerged from the house, Hare snatched a butcher knife and grabbed a haltered horse, a rare possession and prize. *I'm sorry,* he thought briefly. *We're trying to live, too.*

The other men had begun peeling toward the forest, grabbing livestock or barrels of food, some leading horses away as well. Even stale oats were hoarded like treasure.

Then Hare froze. Brown hair flashed in front of his view. Then the man turned, revealing a ripped ear. *Something doesn't feel right.* As he narrowed his eyes, the mass the man was lugging appeared to resemble a person.

No. It can't be.

His thoughts flashed back to his mother, who had been taken away over twenty years prior. Her body still bore faded bruises and the etches of scars. The bald patches on her head. Her fear of men.

Hare screamed at the man, warning him.

The other man stopped briefly. Hare saw the gleam in his chilly eyes, a thousand-yard stare going past him. The girl, probably around his age, was kicking and trying to fight. Hare looked at her face, suddenly realizing how much the girl reminded him of his mother. His vision blurred, warping the world around him and painting it red.

Nobody hurts my mama. No one.

Hare rammed into the other man, disabling him long enough to free the girl. "Run!" he hissed.

The man fired his musket into the air, an explosive blast that resulted in screams of terror and bursts of gunshots. As the men wrestled each other, Hare clawed for his bag, which contained his pocketknife and the looted butcher knife. The man, eyes glimmering with vengeance and teeth gritting in effort, tried to grab his musket. As Hare twisted his head, he saw the girl vanishing into the woods.

Oh no! he thought. *The men are leaving already. I have to leave.* "Let go of me," he growled. "You can still grab something." The man's face was red with effort, his eyes blank. "No," he snarled. "We can die together."

The man grunted, pressing all his strength into Hare's throat, constricting his windpipe. His blue eyes locked with Hare's, sending a chill through his veins. As his vision began to blur, Hare's sight was restricted to the shredded ear as it began to bleed again.

No. I can't die here. You will not kill me.

Throat burning, Hare kneed the man in the ribcage and rolled, grabbing his knife and thrusting it into his attacker's neck. The man collapsed, a pool of blood beginning to form. Bleeding and reaching for his musket, Hare grabbed his rucksack and staggered into the forest.

As the adrenaline gave way to relief, a gunshot rang in the air, the bullet slicing through his shoulder, lodging in his collarbone.

Hare stumbled, then continued to peel into the woods. As he ran, the momentary shock was replaced by an agonizing pain. *Where was Tamar?*

Arriving at the spot where he last saw his mother, Hare desperately whipped his head around the clearing. His mother was nowhere in sight, nor was the man in charge of watching her.

Oh no. Oh no. Oh no. Where could his mother be?

As his blood began to form a pool on the ground, Hare collapsed, vision beginning to blacken. This was it. This was how he was going to die. He felt something coil around him. *Snake!*

"Aghh! Get away from me!" He tried to wriggle free, but his moves were weak and uncoordinated. His eyes met the snake's gleaming red eyes, empty cesspits without matter.

I'm not here to hurt you, the creature hissed. *I am Nehushtan, and I follow souls just as broken as I am. There is no need to fear me. I am forbidden from taking lives when it's not their time. I am not of YHWH, but I must abide by his decrees. The cracks in the world demand a price. Tonight, it will be paid. I will kill you, but only when he allows it.*

With that, the snake slithered away.

Looking around in desperation, the dying man grabbed one of the cloth packs, wringing it around his arm, trying to restrict the blood flow until the world around him became white and the numbness overtook the burning pain.

Forcing his body upright, he stumbled toward the predestined meeting spot.

Half an hour later, Hare crawled into the clearing. The large boulder and stream marked the unmistakable sign for the meeting spot. A few of his men lingered there, bearing baskets of loot and tied animals. *Where were the other men? Where was his mother?*

Upon seeing him and the blood pooling around his body, the men sprinted over, grabbing their friend and hoisting him over the stream. "Where is she?" Hare tried to ask. "Where is everyone else?" Incoherent slurring bubbled from his mouth, his words unable to materialize into speech.

They laid him onto the stone pavement, some cupping water into his mouth, others scrambling for help.

Suddenly, his mother kneeled next to her son. Her fingers lightly brushed his brow, floating across his bruised body. A look of heartbreak spanned her face. Then her arms slumped, empty.

"Mother," Hare tried to garble. "I'm fine. Don't worry."

Blood foamed out instead.

His mother clung to her son, attempting to sing her song of healing that had long gone out of tune.

Dancing across, darkness ebbs in, pulsing out as I call to you, waiting...

Hare felt his body start to lift and his breathing slowing down. The men around him blurred together, the sky turning a golden hue.

Is this what it's like to die?

As the sky turned golden and Hare's body floated in the warm waves of bliss, he saw a black dot in the distance. He did not need to make any effort at all—the waves simply carried him closer to the dot.

The dot enlarged, revealing a lanky woman with long black hair. She gazed at him expectantly, seeming to bounce over the waves.

My child. It is not your time yet. I have the role of bringing souls to paradise and the abyss, but I am not able to take you.

Hare shook his head. "You're mistaken. I died." The woman's lip curved, amused. She shook her head gently.

"Yes," she said. "You did die. But your mother had asked me to replace your life with hers. It was not your time."

Hare's eyes widened as his blood ran cold. "No, no, no! I refuse! My mother can't die!"

The woman wrapped her arms around his. "She has been

dying for a long time. I know you want to protect her, but she will be happy in the Presence. Your work is still incomplete. The next time I see you, it will be different."

Hare still protesting in shock, the woman faded away. *No! No! No!*

Weights materialized on his legs, causing him to sink into the waves. The atmosphere began to grow darker and thicker, the air harder to breathe. His head began to pound and he thrashed around, trying to claw his way back up.

When everything around him darkened into pitch-black, Hare felt his body thud against the stone, hearing the voices of his men chattering in the background.

He was alive.

Mother, what have you done?

Chapter Ten:
The Verdict, A.D. 2555

"Just as no one can be forced into belief, so no one can be forced into unbelief."
—Sigmund Freud

A.D. 2555 – Rocky Mountains, Former Colorado, USA

Hagar woke up with a yelp, body covered with sweat and panting in fear. Almost three years had passed since the Remnant was brutally attacked by vagabonds. Their family home was destroyed, their possessions either stolen or broken as the men fled. Their one goat, which provided them with milk, was taken as well.

That day, Hagar had been walking with her friends and sisters after the daily prayer when beastly shouts began echoing from the forest. The girls had exchanged confused looks. It couldn't be an attack. Their community had not experienced an attack in decades.

The Elders, however, barked orders. "Back to your houses!" they screamed. "Back to your houses now!" As the crowd began to trample and shove back, Hagar lost sight of her peers and family. Where was her father? Her sisters? Swirling veils obscured her view.

Stumbling, Hagar was jostled into the ground, yelping in alarm as the others behind her stepped on her. "Hey!" she wheezed. "Help!"

As the dust faded, Hagar glanced around, her back aching from being crushed by the crowd. As her vision adjusted, she realized with horror that the attackers had begun to ransack houses.

The flurry of veils, the cries of children, and the screams of the women blurred together into her mind. Hagar scrambled up and stumbled, head spinning as she fled to her house.

She tried the door; it was locked. "Father!" she cried. "Let me in!" She called the names of her older sisters: "Mary! Please! Joanna! Esther! Rebekah! Abigail! Dorcas!" She kicked the door, crying. "It's me! Please..." She peered into the window, catching the eyes of Joanna.

Joanna cried, shaking her head. Her father continued to pile furniture in front of the door. "Dad!" she wept. "Don't do this to me." Her father looked away, methodically stacking crates and chairs.

Her head suddenly burst with stars. Falling to the ground in pain, Hagar's body froze as she felt an arm wrap across her neck, and her nearly unconscious body was dragged across the ground.

After the momentary shock, the girl let out a piercing scream, flailing and thrashing. As the arm around her throat tightened, restricting her breathing, Hagar managed to reposition herself and sank her teeth into her captor's flesh. He roared in pain, momentarily dropping her. She whipped around, locking eyes with a large, battered man with one ear completely mangled.

His icy eyes, filled with lust, led Hagar to freeze in terror. As she tried to escape, he grabbed her and rained more blows on her, turning her world black. She felt herself being dragged away, helpless to avoid her fate. Hagar pleaded with the Divine, praying for intervention. *God, please, help me.*

Then she felt herself flying before smashing into the ground. Confused and suffering from a concussion, she woozily raised her head. A young man with sandy-blond hair and intense blue eyes had bowled her attacker over. For a moment, Hagar paused. Uncertain.

"Run!" he hissed at her. Hagar fled into the woods, tripping over branches and stumbling into the creek. She ran until her legs gave way, thudding against a riverbank and bursting into tears.

Hagar stretched her body, her mind wide awake. *Today is the day.* The girl, now with a changing body that indicated womanhood, was aware of the events that would transpire.

A few days ago, Mrs. Elise had pulled Hagar aside, telling

her that Hagar was ready for her mission. "I believe that you have learned everything you could possibly learn from me," she stated. "I will mention this to the Elders."

Yesterday, Mrs. Elise again beckoned Hagar over after the lesson in Algebra. The young woman felt her heart plummet. *I can't do this.* "Hagar," the teacher murmured, "the Elders want to talk with you tomorrow before the Prayer. You will walk to the end of the village, take a sharp right, and then walk near the edge of the forest until you see a boulder. Then you will head straight until you reach a clearing surrounded by willow trees. Wait there and they will call you."

Nodding, Hagar briefly forced a smile to her teacher, went back home, and bawled her eyes out.

A month after the ambush, Hagar's two oldest sisters, Joanna and Mary, had completed their missions. The congregation had prayed over them, Hagar shaking in fear, before they were sent out. Joanna returned a week later, prophesying the rebuilding of the Remnant. Mary had returned after twelve days, in deep meditation and claiming that the Divine God was watching over them. The Elders determined that they both met the Presence.

A week later, Hagar's sisters were married and assigned occupations as a seamstress and village baker.

Two years ago, Esther and Dorcas had completed their missions, along with three boys in their classroom. All of them returned, and the Elders approved Esther and Dorcas for marriage. One of the boys, after an interrogation by the judge, was appointed as a scribe, a sacred and rare role that only the most gifted men were entrusted with.

Last year, Rebekah and Abigail had completed their missions. Rebekah returned after only five days, bringing back visions of a large cataclysmic event happening within the next century. Abigail did not return until over a month later, sparking fear that she would be one of those cursed who never returned. One morning, as the schoolchildren were gazing out the window, one young girl spotted a haggard figure, swaying as she staggered toward the camp.

"Someone's coming!" she screamed. A young boy squinted. "It's Abigail! She returned!" Excited yelps ensued, while Hagar's heart soared. *Abi*, she murmured. *I was scared you would never return.*

Hagar raced toward her sister, who was still stumbling from the dark forest. "Abi!" she yelled. "Abigail!" She was faintly aware of a herd of children also running behind her. Rushing to her sister, she embraced the shaken girl, who was visibly trembling.

Abigail pulled back, startled. Her eyes, marked with deep eye bags, widened. Her long black hair was matted and clumped with dirt.

"Hagar, you mustn't leave, you can't leave for your mission. If you leave, we are all going to die."

The girl recoiled, confused. "Abi," Hagar murmured. "I don't understand what you're saying."

"Nehushtan told me," she whispered. "Hagar, you will kill us all." Then she began to scream maniacally, shaking Hagar.

"Abigail," she stammered urgently. "Who is Nehushtan? What do you mean?" As she attempted to embrace her sister, she felt a sharp explosion of pain. She was bowled over as her sister's hands gripped her airway, choking her. Abigail was frothing.

"You can't leave. Hagar, promise me you won't leave."

The girls were dragged apart by the crowd. Hagar sat, shaking, while her sister continued to screech. "Our camp will be burned to the ground after she leaves! Hagar can't go on her mission! They are going to kill us! A snake told me—it was the serpent from the Garden, she was watching me!"

Hagar blinked, wide-eyed and frozen. Murmurs emerged from the surrounding crowd. She grabbed her protesting sister as the Elders emerged, censorious. Engaged in a hushed conversation, they crowded around the girls. "This child has been possessed by demons!" one declared. "She has gone mad by the Devil." The men grabbed Abigail roughly, gripping her arm.

"Just as the original woman, Eve, was tempted by the serpent to eat the forbidden fruit of the tree, this girl has been tempted and allowed Satan to possess her. She has succumbed to the forces of demons and has brought the evil forces back. Eve tempted her husband, Adam, into eating the forbidden fruit, which caused the Fall of mankind. We must destroy this demon-possessed creature before she infects us. The only way to extinguish this evil is to cast her off the cliff!"

Abigail screamed in terror as the Elders grabbed her, followed by the community. "No! No! No! Don't do this to me! *Please!* I'm not lying!" Hagar's eyes widened in terror as she watched her sisters, hesitant, follow the crowd. Her father gazed away, eyes clouded.

"No!" Hagar screamed. "She is not possessed! She just needs to rest. She didn't mean to attack me!" She grabbed one Elder, who roughly shoved her. "Abigail!"

She shook her father, who continued to stare at the ground. "Father," she implored. "Please save Abigail."

"I have no daughter with that name."

Hagar gaped at her father, terrified at the empty eyes staring back at her. Then she ran, sprinting through the crowd. As she ran toward the cliff, she heard the screams of her sister, painfully crying for help just like she did two years prior. She remembered the icy blue eyes. The bleeding ear. The soft gaze of her unknown savior.

"I'm begging you, I'm innocent! I swear by his name, I'm innocent!"

Hagar cried, a tear dropping to the ground. She heard the rush of the crowd, the growls of anger, the whooshes of robes and skirts gliding against the stone.

As she raised her gaze, she saw the Curtain, just as immovable and imposing as years ago. The colors shone in the sunlight, the cherubim and seraphim gleaming from their stony positions. Silently observing.

"Hagar!" Abigail screamed. "Hagar!"

And just like Abigail had ignored Hagar's pleas for help

years earlier, Hagar closed her eyes as her sister was forced off the cliff, letting out a blood-curdling scream that was abruptly cut short.

Silence.

Hagar bid a farewell to her schoolteacher. The aging Mrs. Elise had taught her for over a decade. "I believe in you," she sighed warmly. "You will do great things."

"I just don't want to end up like …" Hagar paused. "… Abigail."

If the teacher was surprised, her eyes didn't betray her. "Abigail?" she asked blankly. "There was never an Abigail.

"You must be nervous," she told the young woman. "I will pray for your success."

With that, her teacher disappeared into the classroom.

As Hagar left the town, she willed herself to keep walking, ignoring the confusion swamping her mind. When she arrived at the clearing, she waited nervously, legs shaking. Her mind drifted to the death of her sister and how her father had denied his own daughter. She thought about the prophecy her sister had screamed. Her urgent cries, warning her not to leave the camp. *Was she right?* In the distance, Hagar could hear birds faintly chirping and the chitters of crickets.

"Hagar," a deep voice sounded. The girl jumped. Turning around, she saw the twelve Elders standing on a stone platform.

The girl bowed deeply, making sure her veil covered her face. "May the Most Merciful bless you," she murmured.

Heart pounding out of her chest, Hagar waited for their response.

"Come up," one of the Elders commanded.

Bowing once more, Hagar stepped onto the platform.

The Elders were covered in priestly garb with long tassels, their faces obscured with a dark mesh. "We heard that you are ready and have passed your studies," one on the right-hand side stated.

"Praise God for his mercies, I have," she responded.

"Are you ready for your mission?" the Elder in the middle asked her.

Dizzy with fear, Hagar composed herself. "Yes, I am."

She felt the gaze of the twelve Elders piercing through her veil, seeming to bypass the barriers of her heart and scrutinizing every ounce of her being. *Please, please, please, don't find out, don't find out.*

"Very well," one of them said. "We will conduct your mission next Sunday after the Prayer." "We will announce it to the community tomorrow," another chimed in.

"May the LORD bless you and make his face shine upon you," Hagar replied. Bowing for the last time, she turned around and, rounding the corner, fled back to the village.

Will this be my demise? Am I too broken to feel his Presence?

Chapter Eleven:
Calling, A.D. 2000

"Can you pull in Leviathan with a fishhook or tie down its tongue with a rope? Can you put a cord through its nose or pierce its jaw with a hook? Will it keep begging you for mercy? ... Who then is able to stand against me? Who has a claim against me that I must pay? Everything under heaven belongs to me."

—Job 41:1–11 (NIV)

A.D. 2000 – Twin Cities, USA

Hannah felt the breeze of the wind blow across her long black hair. Feeling the rays of the sun probing into her back, she closed her eyes.

Ever since she turned eighteen, the young adult had worked odd jobs, floating around the edges of society. She was twenty-three now, and over the past five years, she had been a bartender, a waitress, an amusement park operator, a mascot for a fast-food joint, and a canvasser for a local roofing company.

Throughout that time, the young woman had been unconsciously, but slowly, healing. At first, the girl would wake up screaming each night and spend much of her time crying or binge-drinking. Time gradually began to heal the broken girl. Hannah had bought an entire library of books to fill her cramped apartment located in the most dangerous part of town.

She had never found *The Curtain*, despite browsing the entire library and inquiring of the staff, who assured her a book like that never existed.

Hannah still had dreams about the mysterious song from over a decade earlier, which occasionally swirled in her head.

Dancing across, darkness ebbs in, pulsing out as I call to you, waiting…

The song no longer scared her. She welcomed the eerie melody, the loneliness of the singer, the brokenness, and hoped that their pleas would be answered by God.

For the past month, Hannah had finally begun to pray and, although irregularly, attend church services again. The words were shaky, but she felt a rare sense of pride in being able to say a simple prayer.

God, I am praying for you to open my heart, to heal me, to help me become the person you want me to be. I know you are there. Amen.

Each time, she would linger in contemplation, hoping for a response.

One particular morning, Hannah decided to escape the mind-numbing repetition of her job, the dull days that blended into the next. She had been working from dawn to dusk, slipping out the door when the sun had not risen and gliding back as it sank into the earth. It was not just for money, but also the welcome relief that the repetitive whirring of the conveyor belt provided. As she stacked and scanned the never-ending wave of packages, the tortured memories and pain that tormented her mind as she tried to sleep would cease, temporarily.

That morning, the sun was warm, with soft rays of light advancing into her dark apartment. Pondering, Hannah strode outside, got into her rusty car, and drove past the manufacturing plant where she worked. There was something she needed to do. Something was calling her, a buzzing sensation within her that continued to reverberate. She drove past winding roads, lush woods, and miles of restricted fencing. The young woman kept her gaze forward, driving until her sputtering car was dangerously low on gas. She stopped at a gas station, refueled, and kept driving. Then refueled again. *Keep going*, a voice whispered. *You aren't there yet. You're so close.*

Only after Hannah reached an inconspicuous spot—a dusty parking lot littered with garbage—did the burning in her heart cease. Beyond the horizon, the sprawling trees blanketed the landscape. Nestled and barely visible in the distance lay the outline of a magnificent waterfall, illuminated by the sunlight. *This*, Hannah thought. *This is where the voices have led me. This is where I will find what I have been searching for my whole life.*

As the day progressed, the young woman steadily trudged through the trails, treading past snapping branches, decaying marsh, and scattered leaves. Her stops for snacks and water became more frequent as her whole body began to ache, shaking with exertion. The waterfall seemed so far, as minuscule as when she had viewed it hours ago in the parking lot. The trails seemed endless, with no human in sight. *You're getting closer*, the voice whispered. *Keep walking.*

As the sun began to set, the woman reached the base of the falls, water rushing over her and colliding into the rocky shores below. Trembling, she sat near the edge and gazed at the rushing water, chest heaving and limbs shaking with exhaustion. As sweat poured down her muddied face, Hannah pondered her life. All her hardships as a child, the difficult years spent in a horrifically dark place, years working night shifts and odd hours to pay rent, the slow healing process from taking medication and going to therapy.

The mass of water sprayed Hannah with chilled droplets that slid down her dust-caked clothes. She idly watched the water tumble thousands of feet down, colliding into rocky ground and slithering through the winding canyon. A thought crossed her mind.

Do I jump? Is life worth living?

She thought about her mother, hanging from the

ceiling. Her father's apathetic response, the miserable nights spent silently crying herself to sleep. Hannah remembered her pillowcase soaked in tears, the song that continually haunted her.

Dancing across, darkness ebbs in, pulsing out as I call to you, waiting...

Shaking her head, she crawled back from the edge to a warm outcropping behind her. The day was so cold. Her jacket was saturated from sitting near the waterfall.

She felt her eyelids grow heavy.

There, at the base of the waterfall, Hannah slipped into a dream.

In her dream, she felt herself in a plain stone clearing with imprints, surrounded by coarse red syenogranite. Dry grass spotted the countryside. Behind her, she saw masses of people gathered together, kneeling prostrate and chanting indistinguishably. But most magnificent was the view across the chasm.

The rolling chasm extended as far as the naked eye could see, the snow-capped mountaintops stretching into the heavens. The trees were magnificently green, the rolling hills below dotted with wildlife. The summits were lustrously white. And the Curtain!

A magnificent curtain stood there, blue and maroon with intricate angel carvings. The cherubim and seraphim appeared exactly like the book she had cherished so many years earlier. The Parochet Curtain of her childhood. She could stare at the velvety blues and reds and the gold angels forever, blissfully ignorant of the world around her.

For the first time in her life, Hannah felt a sense of purpose. There was an uncontrollable call pulling her, a plan etched into her mind.

As she blinked, the beautiful curtain and the vividly decorated drapes disappeared. Dread coursed through her veins. "Oh no," she breathed. *Where have you gone?*

"It's not your time yet," a voice echoed. "Your calling is not complete."

Startled, Hannah woke up, wrapped in bleached blankets in a white room. Tubes stuck into her body fed into a beeping machine. "What happened?" a nurse asked. "A hiker at North Cascades National Park found you unconscious and barely breathing by Colonial Creek Falls. Your driver's license is from Minnesota. Do you realize you're in Washington State?"

"The Curtain," Hannah whispered. "I found her."

For months, Hannah would return from work and comb through maps of mountain ranges, searching for the red syenogranite, snow-capped peaks, and dry grasslands. One day, as she scoured a flier describing the Rocky Mountains, she gasped. *Pikes Peak.* In Colorado. *I found you. I'm coming.*

Hannah had finally found the Mountain.

The next day, the young woman canceled her lease with her landlord, selling everything that she owned. There wasn't much anyway. Her apartment was bare. Her fridge was empty.

Weeks later, loading her aging car with water, food, supplies, and the remaining cash she had left, Hannah filled her car with gas and prepared for the thousand-mile journey to the Rockies. *One more drive. Just hang on one more time.*

For the first time, she felt alive.

I'm coming.

Chapter Twelve:
A Mother's Love, A.D. 2556

"Manuscripts do not burn."

—Mikhail Bulgakov, *The Master and Margarita*

A.D. 2556 – Ciudad Juárez, Former Mexico

Hare rested his head upon the stone slab, the young man engulfed in deep misery. "I love you, Mama," he whispered. "I don't understand. Why?"

Hare had grieved for a long time. He had awoken, days later, to a devastated group of vagrants. To his mother buried in the ground.

Ever since her death, Hare had been trekking, wanting to escape the searing memories that would flash through his mind. The girl's face, filled with terror. The anger in the eyes of the man with the torn ear. The scars that covered his mother. And the snake, whose name he forgot, soundlessly slithering behind. Every time he would turn, the shrubs lightly rustled. Red eyes seemed to bore into his being. Still, Hare never spotted her since that fateful day.

He had left the group, spending the past seasons wandering aimlessly, trekking south. The young man, fleeing his tormentors and the agonies that plagued his mind, welcomed the fair weather, which seemed to warm his lifeless heart. The climate changed from lush mountains to arid desert. He gripped onto the old book he had stolen years prior, the object reminding him of his mother.

Why, Mother? Why?

As he slept one evening, Hare dreamed of his mother for the first time. "Mama!" he choked, running to embrace her. She looked so happy and healthy, reminding him of when he was still in the Meadow. His hands went through Tamar, shocking him.

His mother laughed. "My child, we are in different worlds. Oh, how I've missed you."

"Don't leave, Mother," the son pleaded. "I've missed you so much."

The mother gave her son a wise look. "We will meet again soon, and this time it will be forever." Tamar smiled at her son. "There is a place you must go."

"Where, Mother? What is happening?" Hare shook his head in confusion, bewildered by his situation.

"Even though I do not hold the keys to the future, I

know that you must go there. Do you remember that commune where you almost died?"

A dark chill went through Hare's spine.

"You must go there," his mother continued. "I will guide you from afar. Farewell, my son."

The months following, Hare trekked north, following the faint melody that his mother used to sing, steadily heading over mountains and rivers, valleys and plains.

His dreams increasingly centered around a girl with soft amber eyes, the same girl he had saved years prior. She would beckon him over. *I have something to show you,* she would tell him. As Hare felt his feet float over, he would see the girl fixated on a burning commune scattered with corpses, roasting the bones of all who had died. The wails of grief nearly bowled him over. As he turned to the girl, she would shake her head in sadness. *I wanted to help them, but they wouldn't let me.*

Hare realized that his mission was to find the girl.

The closer Hare got to the commune, the louder the song became:

Dancing across, darkness ebbs in, pulsing out as I call to you, waiting…

Hare had forced himself for years to head south, swimming upstream against the conscience of his mind. Turning north, he quickened his pace, heading toward the mountains he had dreaded for so long. His internal compass oscillated northward, pointing to the girl, to where he had buried his heart and conscience. Now she just had to hold on.

I'm coming. Mother, I'm coming home.

Chapter Thirteen:
The Deception of Women, 3500 B.C.?

"Better to reign in Hell than to serve in Heaven."
—John Milton, *Paradise Lost, Book II*

3500 B.C.? – Ancient Mesopotamia, Former Iraq

The woman padded through the Garden, silently observing the idyllic scenery. Birds chirped and warbled, and the bushes rustled with life. Lush vines wrapped around thick tree trunks, the leaves devoid of pest infections and diseases. If death was the absence of life, there was no life. Only pure, unadulterated existence.

It was in this existence where the woman was created, molded by the Most High into a suitable mate for the man.

Bathing by the Pishon, the red-haired woman soaked her long hair in the clear stream. Trepidation expanded as she realized what was to happen. Dusting the leaves from her body, she padded into the forest, embracing the warmth cast by the light. Walking into the midst of the Garden, in her designated meeting spot with the man, the woman sat below a weeping willow tree whose long leaves traced the stone platform below. *What would she say to the Most High?*

She sensed the man long before he arrived. The sounds of cracking branches grew louder. The sound of birdsong faded.

The man strode into the enclosure, eyes boring into her body. Closing her eyes, Lilith let her body intertwine with his, silently echoing his movements. As they began to enmesh their bodies together, the woman willed herself to open her eyes, to run her hands across his body, to move her body along with his, like an instrument in motion. She felt his seed enter her body, sensed entwining within her womb.

She felt empty, dull resentment brewing in her soul.

After, the man pulled himself up, his eyes riddled with confusion.

As the sun dawned and the man and woman awaited the Most High, the animals joined them in anticipation. Many had already borne offspring, smaller creatures that clung to their mothers and suckled gently.

As the Presence arrived, he seemed to settle in front of the woman. She felt his gaze pierce through her soul. "I'm sorry," she whispered.

"It is your soul," the Voice said. "I have given you free will."

"What do I do?" she asked. "I know I am disappointing you."

"That is for you to find out," came the reply.

As the Presence ascended into heaven, the woman pondered.

The woman began to have strange visions of herself morphing into a hideous creature without legs, joining a legion of other similarly monstrous beings and slithering across a dark expanse. She would be lifted, hissing in fury, then bolted into a spike. Her vision would be glazed red, covering the world around her in a sickly bright substance. *Blood.*

As her stomach began to grow, the woman sensed a sea of anger rising within her. She did not dislike the man but despised him. She felt anger toward the Creator, whose all-knowing gaze collected her thoughts but did nothing.

One night, as she felt birth pangs and the kicks of her unborn child, the woman sighed, hands running through her hair. "I should feel happy," she sighed. "Why do I feel so broken?"

Gazing across the riverbank, the woman closed her eyes, imagining her future in the Garden. There was no shortage of abundance, each tree bearing ripe and sweet fruit, the sun always warm, the Most High always gracious.

That night, something inside her soul irreparably snapped.

The day for childbirth came. The man crouched next to her, fascinated and terrified as the contractions began.

For the first time, Lilith felt her water break, her child slipping out. Her husband cried with joy, praising the Most High.

That night, the woman killed her child, silently smothering him while the man slept. Then she left his lifeless body and sat by the river. Waiting for the inevitable. As she washed, the water stained red.

As the Presence began to descend, the woman fell to her knees, pleading with the Most High to have mercy on her.

The atmosphere filled with rage, the Almighty wrathfully turning on the woman. *What have you done?*

Trembling with fear, Lilith squeezed her eyes shut.

Lilith felt waves of fury slamming into her, rolling her around, the blood of her child suffocating her and squeezing her empty. When the Presence cleared, what remained of the beautiful woman was a large serpent with red eyes. Nehushtan.

In pain, the serpent dragged herself into the dark depths of the Garden. As the years passed into decades and centuries, Nehushtan would watch in seclusion as another partner was fashioned from the man, his rib bone being molded into another woman that bore resemblance to her previous body. She watched the man slowly forget about her and smoldered as she saw him and the new woman make love. Lovingly named Eve, the woman had innocent eyes that gleamed with curiosity, the same gaze that the serpent had once held. Eve was to become *havva*, the source of life for the man. Yet Nehushtan saw her weakness, her affinity towards the impermissible. Her longing glimpses towards the Tree of Knowledge.

The snake observed the woman being slowly entranced by the Forbidden Fruit. She whispered temptations, entering her mind.

And she was the one who convinced the woman to eat the Forbidden Fruit, hissing in pleasure as the man ate the fruit as well. Finally, he would feel her desolation, her despair. He had left Lilith after her damnation. Now, Nehushtan impassively observed as the man lost everything.

Nehushtan's red eyes gleamed as the Most High destroyed the Sacred Garden, cursing the woman and her descendants with painful childbirth. Their offspring would be descendants of the man, tangible tokens of the serpent's former love, her stifled matrimony within a lifeless cage. The snake would spend centuries silently trailing the man's offspring, now cursed with the afflictions of mortality.

As the Most High cursed mankind, destroying Nehushtan's legs, the serpent felt a pang of pride. Now everyone felt the pain she felt. She was not afraid of the Most High. She would not know that she was cursed with immortality, reincarnating through various serpent forms, fated to slither across the earth in search of broken souls. Nor would the serpent know that she would be nailed onto a stake by Israel's first prophet and destroyed centuries later following pagan worship of her form.

She was cursed to live. Forced to eternally exist in misery until she was finally allowed to die.

All she was aware of was her emptiness.

The man will crush your head, and you will strike his heel.

Chapter Fourteen: Judgment, A.D. 2555

"For now we see only a reflection as in a mirror; then we shall see face to face. Now I know in part; then I shall know fully, even as I am fully known."
—1 Corinthians 13:10 (NIV)

A.D. 2555 – Former Rocky Mountains, USA

"We pray, today, that the Almighty Divine will bestow his favor upon this child, Hagar. God, have mercy on us! Jesus, Son of David, have mercy on her."

With that, Hagar had walked, her back turned to her only home, into the forest. She had been unable to sleep the entire first night, but now her body tingled with nerves.

The first few days, the girl had spent her time catching fish in the streams and trying to meditate.

Jesus, Son of David, have mercy on me. Jesus, Son of David, have mercy on me. Jesus, Son of David, have mercy on me.

After a week, the girl was growing desperate, knowing her time was running out. "God," she cried into the night. "I know you are there!" She wept. "Please, just answer this prayer."

Hagar tried to make up an answer, tried to imagine what God would tell her.

Nothing came.

As the days wore past, Hagar contemplated returning and creating an elaborate story. Then she remembered the fate of Abigail, who had been driven off the cliff. She had warned Hagar, yet Hagar still left.

Hagar was now covered in ticks. Her clothes were ragged, and she no longer had the motivation to eat or move. She spent her days curled in a tight ball, blankly staring at the unknown. Waiting to die.

The days blurred together. Months came and passed. The young woman foraged for berries and clumsily used the skills her father taught her to spear fish and trap rabbits. As the seasons came and passed, Hagar grew weaker. Soon, she spent the days in and out of consciousness. The young woman no longer knew when she was lucid or hallucinating. The trees blurred into each other. Abigail would talk to her, and the ground would become engulfed in flames. Hagar saw her village being raided, her family cornered by a mass of men and bayoneted into pieces. Horrified, Hagar screamed for Abigail and her sisters. But she had become mute.

One night, as fever raged through her body, the rain

began to pound, covering the girl with sludge. Hagar attempted to scramble away, but her arms gave out, sliding into the muck. Her head rang as it struck against a stone. Her body stilled.

"Hagar," someone whispered. "My daughter."

The girl couldn't move. *Who was that?* "Mother," she whispered. "Is that you?"

"I am sorry I was not able to raise you. My daughter, you have done so well."

"Mother," Hagar breathed. "I've waited so long." *I'm dying.* She waited, welcoming the arms of death.

"I've always been with you. I am here. And I will always be watching."

Hagar felt warmth wrap around her body as her mother embraced her. She tried opening her eyes.

Then overwhelming waves of delirium engulfed the girl, continuously wracking Hagar until she no longer knew what was real.

Mother?

Stillness.

She could move. Hagar forced her eyes open, her hazy vision forming a blurry face. "Mother? Am I dead?" No sound came out.

When Hagar opened her eyes again, trembling, her vision cleared and the man who had saved her years prior emerged from the dim light, arms wrapped around her shaking body,

The Curtain Between Us

eyes rounded in concern.

That man, with his unmistakable sky-blue eyes and sandy-blond hair, hovered over her. She felt her body being suspended into the air, a warm blanket covering her, hot liquid spooned into her throat.

Am I dead? Where's Mother?

She saw the man more and more between blacking out. His soft blue eyes, narrowed in concern. His long hair, falling and blocking his gaze. The hot liquid that would slide down her throat each time.

The days became longer and longer. One day, Hagar realized that she was alive. The man who had saved her years prior had saved her again.

As she tried to talk, her words gurgling, the man shushed her. "I'm Hare," he told her gently. "I know you remember me. I won't hurt you."

Hare told Hagar about his childhood, his upbringing in the meadows, his mother's story, his years with the vagabonds, how he died and was saved by his mother. He told the woman about his dream that led him to her. And, most importantly, he told her how he was going to find his mother's previous home, the farm from before she was kidnapped.

"What is your name?" he asked gently.

Hagar grabbed a stick, etching the word H A G A R onto the stone. The man looked at her, confused. "I can't read," he admitted sheepishly.

She tried to mouth *Hagar*, but the words couldn't come

out. She was mute.

As Hagar recovered, she began to trail Hare. "Are you sure you want to follow me?" the man asked. "I'm not even sure where I'm going." The girl smiled and nodded. There was no other place she could go.

For the next few months, Hagar and Hare wandered the woods together. Although Hagar wasn't able to speak, Hare filled the silence with his chatter. Hagar grew to enjoy his presence and company.

"We're heading to the farm where my mother grew up. Her name was Tamar, and she was so beautiful. She sacrificed her life for me. She told me so many stories. Her ancestors had stored all their books in a cave by the farm. It's still there, and we can add this book."

Along with them, Hare had brought the copy of the *Holy Bible*, a book that Hagar had latched onto. She tried to draw out the stories, but to no avail.

Hagar began to see a large snake with red eyes trailing them. Each time she grabbed Hare and pointed toward the serpent, the creature always managed to disappear before he saw it.

Child, the animal hissed. *He can't see me.*

As they trekked further west, the man and woman began to develop feelings for each other. Hare began to stroke the woman's long hair, finding flowers to make a beautiful flower crown. Hagar would finger the man's soft hair and clasp onto his warm arms when she thought he had fallen asleep. They began to embrace each other for warmth as nights grew frigid. Fleeting touches progressed into lingering caresses. One night, as the moon began to wane, they made love under the starry sky.

All of their lives, the man and woman had been alone, buffeted by the bitter winds of cruel fate and isolated within their own adverse communities. Swimming against a pummeling tide of fate, they had only known death and loss, destruction and the numbing cold of solitude. That night, as their bodies entwined, the man and woman discovered the warmth of love and the presence of each other's undiluted passion—their two strands woven as one.

The intimacy of love, it seems, brings color to a bleached canvas, a flicker of light in an otherwise wretched existence.

Chapter Fifteen:
Peace at Last, A.D. 2007

"But who prays for Satan? Who in eighteen centuries, has had the common humanity to pray for the one sinner that needed it most, our one fellow and brother who most needed a friend yet had not a single one, the one sinner among us all who had the highest and clearest right to every Christian's daily and nightly prayers, for the plain and unassailable reason that his was the first and greatest need, he being among sinners the supremest?"
—Mark Twain, Letter XI, *Letters from the Earth*

A.D. 2007 – Pikes Peak, USA

Hannah groaned with pain, her muscles cramping from overextension. She had been hiking for the past few weeks, following her compass to the base of the Rockies.

The packs of food and water she had packed were almost depleted, her sleeping bag ragged and torn from the rocky terrain. Hannah was almost certain that she would be classified as a missing person. But there was nobody who could report her. She had no family or friends.

As her feet trudged up the mountain, Hannah began to crawl, slowly pulling her body up near the edge. She was so close. She knew it.

Rain began to patter from the sky, the dirt road under Hannah turning into sticky mud. Her body became caked with it, slipping each time she tried to crawl up.

The sky darkened, and the light drizzle was replaced by a deluge of rain. Hannah felt her grip slip and her body begin to slide down the trail. *All the effort. Gone. I'll die like this and nobody will remember me.*

A tear slid down her cheek. Then the tears began to flow. Hannah sobbed in agony, crying as her dream began to float away. Her life, it seemed, had amounted to nothing. All the pain she endured was in vain.

Please. God, help me.

As she was about to close her eyes and give up, preparing to slip off the cliff, Hannah saw a snake slither toward her. Its glowing red eyes gleamed at her empathetically. *My poor child,* it hissed. *You're broken, too.*

The young woman let out a guttural wail, the years of silent torment and agony released like a volcano, with mountains of fire erupting after centuries of complacency. *Mother, are you watching me? I need your help.*

Hannah closed her eyes.

The rain began to slow, then stopped.

She felt an envelope of warmth surrounding her. *Hannah, my daughter, you've been so brave.*

The young woman felt her body relax, her soul rising out

of her body. As she looked around, she saw the magnificent chasm and the beautiful Curtain adorned with cherubim. The angels seemed to beckon her. Even the blue and red fabrics were tangibly soft, glowing with light. It was so large, so grand and breathtakingly beautiful.

A Curtain, symbolic of the distance she felt from a Higher Power, now stood tall and strong, beaming its splendor for all to see.

"It is so beautiful," she breathed. "But where did it come from?"

It has been waiting for you. Now, you can finally be at peace. Come, your time is here.

Breathing deeply, the woman stepped into the light.

Chapter Sixteen:
Warmth, A.D. 2558

"The only thing worse than a boy who hates you: a boy that loves you."
—Mark Zusak, *The Book Thief*

A.D. 2558 – Former Battle Mountain, Nevada

Hare awakened, stretching his sore body. The girl was curled next to him, still snoring. He smiled, his heart filling with love for the beautiful girl at his side. "Shhhh," he murmured. "We're almost here." The girl blinked. Her soft amber eyes gazed warmly at him. Yawning, she pushed herself out of their makeshift enclosure. Then, she leaned over, smiled, and kissed him.

Hare's stomach danced with butterflies. The young man was not even sure if the girl understood where they were going. But she stuck near him, matching his step pace by pace, her smile and trusting eyes warming his heart. *Is this what love feels like?*

As they packed their belongings, Hare explained the situation. All the landmarks his mother described seemed to lead to this place. They had been traveling west, then north, following the mountains that loomed around them. The landscape reminded him of years ago, during the attack on the former camp, the days in the mountains. The death of his mother. Finding her. As the feeling grew stronger, Hare became certain. It seemed that the farm should be past the woods, lodged between the peaks of a mountain. They should arrive there by tonight.

"I'll be right back," he whispered, heading out to snare some rabbits. The wind whistled through the trees, light green leaves fluttering in the air. Birds chirped while the bushes rustled with life. Hours passed as the boy carefully began to set the traps. As he was strolling back, he saw a hare bound in front of him, followed by a red snake. Suddenly, Hare felt a cold chill run through his body. Something was terribly wrong. *Was that his mother's voice?*

Run, my son.

Hare sprinted toward the enclosure, lungs burning. As he neared, there was a tortured scream. Pushing through, he saw the girl in the middle of the enclosure, a serpent with fangs wrapped around her body. A snake. "No!" he roared. "Don't hurt her!"

No one can hurt her.

The serpent bared its fangs, rising high into the air, ruby eyes gleaming. Hare gasped, his breath shuddering. It was the same serpent from Chicago, the same eyes as the one that encircled him after he'd been shot by the man with a torn ear. *Nehushtan.*

Don't come closer, Hagar tried to scream. *The snake is luring you!*

The outskirts of her vision began to swirl and mix together into a bloody hue as the snake began to constrict.

The girl wept silently, shaking her head while tears dropped to the parched ground. *Please, don't come. She won't hurt me.*

Grabbing his pocketknife, Hare rushed the serpent. He thrust his blade into the snake, feeling the sharp blade make a connection with solid flesh. The creature let out a monstrous roar of agony while its poisonous fangs latched onto his neck.

He will crush your head, and you will strike his heel.

Hare gasped for breath, the fatal poison working its way through his system. His hands, quivering, grasped the blade tighter. He plunged the blade deeper, twisting meat into fleshy carnage. With a final shove, Hare limply collided with the gravelly ground.

He felt the girl shaking him, her body embracing him, her lips finding his. Hare saw the dead body of the serpent, gushing blood, forming a pool near the carcass. The red eyes that had haunted him for so long stared blankly at him.

"I'm sorry," he whispered. "I love you." But the words wouldn't form. His breaths began to gurgle into desperate gasps for air.

I'm not here to hurt you. I am Nehushtan and I follow souls just as broken as I am. There is no need to fear me. I am forbidden from taking lives when it's not their time. I am not of YHWH but I must abide by his decrees. I will kill you, but only when he allows it.

His body began to float, drifting upward toward a bright, sunny meadow.

The familiar woman welcomed him, her long black hair blowing in the breeze.

"Welcome," she said. "Your mother is waiting for you."

"What about the girl?" Hare asked. "Will she be alright?"

"Don't worry about her." The woman smiled. "She has her own journey ahead, but yours is over."

Hagar wept, embracing the cold body of her only friend. "Why?" she murmured mutely. "I told you not to come for me. Wake up." She shook him. "We're almost there." She sobbed, emitting guttural wails that echoed through the empty forest. The girl kissed the boy, willing the Almighty to resurrect him, to bring life into a lifeless body.

Hare, what have you done? Why did you leave me?

Their possessions were haphazardly scattered around the clearing. The dead body of the snake was stiff, its empty red eyes gazing lifelessly into the abyss.

"Hare," she breathed. "I loved you."

He was so close, yet so far.

Hagar had lost her community, her family, and now, her

only friend.

She was alone in the wilderness with her dead beloved, who had sacrificed his life for a nameless girl from his dreams.

The young woman hung her head.

Dancing across, darkness ebbs in, pulsing out as I call to you, waiting...

Hearing the strange melody, the heartbroken girl raised her head in confusion.

Follow me, the voice seemed to be saying. *I will help you.*

"Hare," she breathed silently. "I can't leave you." A warm spirit circled around her, murmuring. *He is taken care of. He is at peace now.*

Eyes full of longing, Hagar embraced her love one last time. Then she turned around and chased after the voice. Hagar was led through the mountains, past plains, and finally, to the brink of the farm. She gripped the Bible, remembering what Hare told her.

Books and their ideas never die. If these books survive, maybe in the future, others will be able to pierce our story so our lives won't be in vain.

Hagar stepped outside the forest onto a ledge. Across from her stood a farm, exactly how Hare had told her. There was a clear lake at the foot of the mountains. The wood of the farmhouse was peeling, and the once-bright-red hue on the walls had long faded, but it still stood tall. Animals grazed at the bottom by the lake. There was a pump, and fruit trees dotted the landscape.

It was beautiful.

"I must leave now," the spirit breathed. "My mission has not been completed yet, but yours ends here."

As Hagar looked back one last time, she saw the faint outline of a woman with black eyes.

"Can I ask you something?" Hagar mouthed. Although no words came out, the Spirit paused, then turned. "What is your name? I never asked you."

There was a pause.

"Hannah. My name is Hannah."

Chapter Seventeen:
A Case Study, Translated into Twenty-First-Century English Vernacular, A.D. 3508

"A great book should leave you with many experiences, and slightly exhausted at the end. You live several lives while reading."
—William Styron

BEGINNING OF DOCUMENT

The Third World War, although most of the context was lost in the explosions and the aftermath, resulted in the complete utilization of the world's collective nuclear arsenal.

What occurred for over one thousand years after was complete darkness: the Dark Ages, wherein most of the population was eradicated. Those that survived the bombs and their aftermath were often in the rural areas of the world. They did not have any access to technology, as everything was wiped out in the explosions.

There were massacres waged over scarce resources. Many religious people believed it was the end of the world. And in a sense, it was.

Unfortunately, most of the world's books and historical documents were lost. However, archeologists are currently unearthing preserved books concealed in inconspicuous caverns, many of which have not been found elsewhere. In the western rocky mountaintop caves of the former United States, well-preserved copies of the Bible; Quran; Hindu Vedas; Homer's *Odyssey*; Sun Tzu's *Art of War*; Nietzsche's writings; and the musings of Tolstoy, Cervantes, Twain, Shakespeare, Alcott, Murakami, Orwell, and Fitzgerald were stored and maintained. These books seem to have been conserved with great care and are in remarkably pristine condition. Though it is impossible to determine the preserver of the artifacts, they have provided a glimpse into the past history and religions that many adhered to.

Strangely, in the Rocky Mountains, near the sprawling cliffs of Pikes Peak, there lies a former encampment of an isolated community that likely housed around three thousand individuals at its peak. There, many copies of the Bible were translated and maintained. Across the chasm, there was also a peculiar monument of a Curtain, well-maintained and crafted over a multitude of years. Now it stands, tattered and faded, a shadow of its former glory. The Curtain appears to be multicolored. There also seem to be figures etched into the piece, but time has worn out the distinguishable details.

The Curtain Between Us

In the midst of their living encampment, a multitude of scattered corpses were dated to the same epoch, most bearing blunt-force trauma, suggesting that the group was simultaneously massacred by outside forces. There also appear to be the remains of individuals at the bottom of the chasm, many dating far before the supposed massacre.

Farther away, near the ruins of what was formerly Battle Mountain in Nevada, an old mining town once inhabited by the Northern Paiute, Shoshone, and Washoe tribes, lay the ruins of a farm with one of the only completely preserved Bibles.

Strangely, the bleak landscape surrounding the farm is interrupted by a field of white lilies, a species not native to the area. Scrawny brown hares are also abundant in the countryside, recognizable by their bushy tails and bright eyes.

Although these events seem rather peculiar, they hold the stories of individuals long ago.

After all, my readers, reality is often stranger than fiction.

END

ACKNOWLEDGMENTS

From the bottom of my heart, I am so grateful to everyone who has made this book possible. Thank you to Sophie Eigen, for your thoughts and initial revisions to my first manuscript. I am also especially appreciative of my family, and to my parents, who have voyaged from the other end of the Earth so I can travel this step. Mom, Dad, I love you more than words can express. To my grandma, who raised me in a foreign country, with a language she never learned: Thank you for sacrificing the comfort of your old age and retirement for your grandchildren. I love you (奶奶，我爱你). I am so, so thankful to Wendy Haavisto, my Legislative Assistant at the Minnesota Senate, who provided me with encouragement and gave me the strength to journey on. I am endlessly indebted to you. I extend my appreciation to Senator Gary Dahms, who I had the joy to intern for during the 2025 Legislative Session. I admire your service to the people of Minnesota's 15th District. Senator, you stoked a flame within me for public service.

Thank you to Dr. Matthew Miller and Professor Leanna

Swanson at the University of Northwestern - St. Paul. Your genuine care and support has been a vital line of support during my collegiate journey, and I have grown so much in my writing under your watchful eyes. I also send my love to Dr. Adina Kelley; her husband, Professor Samuel Kelley; and their two children, Benjamin and Lydia. Dr. Kelley, you fought so hard, and I owe so much of my story to your love and flaming passion for American history. Your story has made it into my story.

In addition, I thank my proofreaders, Aubrielle Manthey, Reese Gorney, Katelyn Rens, and my sweetest Mari Evans, for your diligent and painstaking work of combing through this book. Your efforts in polishing my manuscript are truly appreciated.

I am so appreciative towards my erhu teacher, Wei Ming Chiang, as well as Ms. Aileen Chan. Your dedication to the classical Chinese snakeskin instrument has cultivated a lifelong love of music, coaxing hauntingly mysterious melodies out of two strings. Your belief in me formed the melodies that drift across the pages of this book.

Lastly, I stand in absolute reverence to the Almighty, who has led me out of the darkness and into His marvelous light.